SOMEWHERE IN CALIFORNIA

SOMEWHERE SERIES, BOOK 3

TOBY JANE

CHAPTER ONE

Jade

Standing in front of the TV judges of *Dance, Dance, Dance*, my meager file of credits open in front of them, I wish I'd done something jazzier with my hair than a bun. I'm dressed in the traditional pale pink of ballet workout clothing: tights, a leotard, ballet slippers, a filmy wrap skirt, and my own signature touch, a wide black velvet ribbon tied around my waist.

The ribbon provides a focal point for the eye when I do my audition—and I need to stand out. But a ribbon isn't much of a statement for a dancer now that it's 1992, and Madonna is our style icon. I'm definitely in over my head with this tryout.

"Thank you for joining us, Miss Michaels," one of the judges says. She has the slender build and upright posture of a retired professional.

"Jade, please."

"According to this, Jade, you began dancing at fourteen. Are you aware that's late for a professional career?"

"Yes. I grew up on Saint Thomas in the Virgin Islands. There was nowhere to dance where I lived. My family moved to California when I was fourteen, and that's when I started dancing."

"Ah. So tell us what you're going to be performing."

"Just a short piece from *The Nutcracker*. With adaptations."

"You're aware this audition is for a competitive television show that includes a variety of styles—not just classical ballet?" The male judge is a harshly handsome middle-aged man crowned with a green Mohawk, wearing an armful of jingling copper bracelets. I can feel the eye of the TV camera boring into my back right between my shoulder blades. I ignore the blinking red light of the camera in front of me.

"Yes, sir. I said 'with adaptations,' didn't I?" I smile as big and charming as I can.

People have told me I ought to smile more, that I'm almost as pretty as my sister Pearl Michaels, the supermodel, when I smile. That's a stretch, but it seems to help, because the grumpy male judge inclines his head and flicks a finger for the music. My favorite song, *Total Eclipse of the Heart*, comes on.

I drop to the ground, folding in tight on myself.

The song's a little old, but it speaks to me. Speaks to what I long for—a love so big it sweeps me away. In the secret of the studio where I've been dancing and giving lessons for the last five years, I've choreographed my own routine to it.

As the music builds, I slide my legs out from beneath my upper body into full splits, then, pointing my toes, using only leg strength, I draw my legs together so that my arched upper torso lifts from the ground by main force. I hear a gasp from one of the female judges at this maneuver, but the music's changing, and I fling my arms wide and spin, doing ten rotations, then exit into a moonwalk. From there I segue into the breakdance sequence, doing upper body pop and lock, shuffling with rubber legs, and an Egyptian maneuver with my rib cage as my 'heart' beating in exaggerated twitches beneath my hand. That brings another surprised exclamation from someone.

But I can't hope, or think, because next comes the laid-back leap extension across the stage, and the pirouette, and the mime-in-the-box followed by the sassy hip shake of my best cha-cha.

I'm waiting for the buzzer to end my audition. I've watched this show every season, and hopeful contestants never seem to make it through a full minute of dancing, so I didn't choreograph more than two minutes.

But the buzzer doesn't sound, so I dance on: flinging myself into whatever feels right in the moment, a collage of moves I've perfected...and finally Bonnie Tyler cries her *total eclipse of the heart*, and I sink into a deep curtsy, heaving for breath and dripping with sweat.

When I rise, the judges are standing. Applauding.

The eye of the TV camera zooms in on my face, capturing my mouth falling open and tears welling, because my heart has just been totally eclipsed by the dance.

"Congratulations," the male judge says, grinning so wide I don't recognize him. "You've got a golden ticket. You're going to LA!"

My legs won't hold me up anymore. I sink to the floor in a weepy puddle.

Someone comes to help, lifting me up from beneath my limp arm, looping it over his shoulder and helping me out of the audition area. He settles me onto a hard plastic chair backstage.

"Here," he says. "Jade Star Michaels." He hands me a piece of soft fabric, and I mop my streaming face and blow my nose on it. "That was amazing."

"Thanks," I say, muffled in the material. "What is this?" Real cloth feels silky and expensive under my hands.

"Handkerchief. You can give it back another day."

I look up into the face that belongs to such a kind voice. He's handsome: short dark blond hair, light hazel eyes, a mouth made of angles and curves.

"How did you know my name?"

The man holds up a clipboard. "I'm the main producer. Brandon Forbes." He looks at me intently. "And I knew your sister."

"Which one?" I ask, honking my nose again. I spot his initials stitched onto the corner of the handkerchief. "I have two." Neither of my sisters, nor my mom, knows that I'm here in San Francisco at this audition.

"Pearl and I dated at one time. Did she ever mention me?"

"No, I'm sorry. We're not close."

Forbes's mouth tightens with a twist that looks like old pain. "Well. It was a long time ago."

"Yeah. She's married now." I don't want to talk about his relationship with my supermodel sister. I stand up. "Thanks for the help. That was... overwhelming. I didn't expect to have to dance the whole song."

"It's never happened before," Forbes says, eyes bright. He seems to be really seeing me for the first time. "You were really something out there. How old are you?"

"Twenty. And thanks for this." I want to hand the kerchief back to him, but it's gross. I'm going to have to wash it before I return it. I can feel the urge to get the germs off my hands plucking at my nerves. "What happens now?"

"Here's your golden ticket." Forbes hands me a small packet. It's topped by a gold foil ticket that reads, *"You're invited to the next level of competition in Los Angeles!"* Clipped onto the back are vouchers for United Airlines, a couple of taxi rides, and a Holiday Inn. "Stick around. Watch the rest of the competition. And be at Universal Studios in Los Angeles next Tuesday."

"I'll be there. With bells on," I shake one of my ankles, where I've tied a little silver bell.

"Nice." Forbes pats my head like I'm three. "See you around."

"You will." Pearl Moon Michaels isn't going to be the only famous name in our family.

Brandon

Meeting Jade Michaels at the auditions was a punch to the gut.

The girl is an amazing dancer. Looking down at where I've jotted my own homemade ratings on our roster of competitors, she's one of our strongest contestants so far.

Slender and small-boned, she's built with the long legs and short torso that are ideal for ballet. Long auburn hair and green eyes make her distinctive. The only feature she shares with her heartbreaker sister Pearl is a mouth made for kissing.

Pearl. Five foot nine inches of blue-eyed, blonde perfection. I helped make Pearl the supermodel she is. I held her in my arms, saved her from a mugger—and hoped for more. But it wasn't to be. She met and married someone whose shadows blended with hers—someone more suited to her streak of darkness. I get that now.

I shake my head to clear it, and click on my handheld radio. "How many more contestants are we running today?"

Throwing myself back into work helps me move on from the disorienting encounter. I've found my niche in my mother's media empire by starting the dance show. We're in our third season and only getting more popular. Our outreaches to cities outside of LA were yielding a great crop of talent, and The Melissa Agency was doing a brisk business signing some of the best performers in the country. The rest of the day into afternoon passes in a blur of phone calls to the rest of my staff, solving ongoing issues with the camera feeds, and prepping for our return to LA next week and the next phase of the competition.

But I can't stop thinking about Pearl, and Jade, and the emptiness Pearl left behind—an emptiness that I try to fill with work and women. None of it lasts long.

I return to my room at the Fairmont Hotel, but can't relax. I need to work out. I head down to the hotel's gym and push weights. Even with my Walkman blasting, it isn't enough. I slide my room key into my pocket and leave the hotel for a run.

The stately landmark hotel is near the center of the city on one of its highest points, so I head downhill, angling across streets, Nikes thumping on the sidewalk as I pass coffee shops, clothing boutiques, and multi-ethnic crowds going about their business. I make my way to Ocean Beach like a salmon going to the sea.

On that great, fog-wreathed stretch of sand I breathe easier, running on the hard-packed edge near the water.

I'm over Pearl.

At least I'd thought so. But seeing her sister has made me wonder.

It's not like I've been a monk since Pearl dumped me after one of her fashion shows four years ago. I'm surrounded by beautiful women, many of them trying to get some advantage in a tough industry by cozying up to me—or my mother.

I learned to spot that gleam in the eye of a pretty girl long ago: the furtive passing of a phone number followed by the pressure to put a word in with Melissa: "Can you just show her this photo?"

I'm no angel. I've taken a few up on what was offered. But Pearl was the first model I'd ever "discovered" myself. That time, the shoe was on the other foot—I wanted Pearl to see me as her knight in shining armor, not only chasing off a mugger that I interrupted robbing her, but giving her a break she'd never have had without me.

I was the one who ended up falling in love. I should never have let myself get sucked in that way. I never even slept with her, damn it, and still somehow fell for her like the proverbial ton of bricks—more fool me.

I run harder in my frustration. Finally, returning to the hotel, I shower and call Melissa for the weekly check-in she's requested as part of our partnership.

"Hello, son." Her voice is cool. I hear the tinkling of ice cubes in her evening cocktail.

I've poured myself a drink too, and put my feet up on the hotel's striped ottoman, looking out at the lighted Golden Gate through a triptych of long windows. "Hello, Mother. This is your weekly update call."

"I assumed as much. What's new in the dance show business?"

"We've had a great series of tryouts here in San Francisco. Glad this part is over. A new city every week is more exhausting than glamorous."

"You don't have to tell me. Any new talent worth mentioning?"

"Yeah. Jade Star Michaels." The name pops out of my mouth without my intention.

A long pause. I envision my mother's golden-green eyes tighten the way they do when she hears something she doesn't particularly like. "As in...sister of Pearl Michaels?"

"That's right. Phenomenal dancer." My mind's eye fills with the memory of Jade's mish-mash of styles set to *Total Eclipse of the Heart*. "Huge emotion, passion, and technical ability. Her tryout was the first one to ever last the length of a song. Of course, she's continuing on to compete in LA."

Another pause. "Any runway talent there?" Melissa's way of asking me if famous Pearl's sister has any potential as a model.

"Don't think so. Too short." I swirl the cubes in my drink in agitation. I don't want Melissa getting her hooks into Jade. Poor kid—naïve and innocent, not like Pearl at all.

"What about print work? Pearl's got so much charisma. If Jade has even a fourth of that, she'll be great for magazine ads."

"Don't know," I growl. "Move on, Mother." She never lets me call her anything but Melissa. I wait for the rebuke, but it never comes. Maybe she's mellowing. "Our stock is up. If we get the numbers we're going for this quarter, I think it will be time to finally go public."

We've been negotiating to buy an entire TV network that we could then produce content for, including preferential spots for commercials involving The Melissa Agency's client base.

"Keep me posted," she says, and we wrap up the conversation. "I'm worried about you, son."

I'm startled. Melissa doesn't go there with me, that whole touchy-feely bit isn't part of our dynamic. "What are you worried about?"

"That you will get—I don't know. Burned out. You used to want to be an engineer, remember?"

How could I forget? I'd been a student at MIT when I discovered Pearl. Melissa used that situation to lure me back into the business with financial incentives too sweet to ignore. "I need you," she'd finally said. "I'm not getting any younger, and to take this business to the next level, I need someone at my side that I can trust."

I changed my major to business administration, and developed the TV arm of the business, my own project. I found it surprisingly fulfilling. "Water under the bridge. I'm happy doing what I'm doing."

"Well, don't forget to have a little fun. Go out. I want you to meet someone special."

"You got it, Boss."

I hang up the hotel's gilt-edged phone. I'm still restless. I want to see the film from today's tryouts. I pick the phone up and call Alan Bowes, the show's director, a short fireplug of a bald man who wears nothing but black leather and a lot of energy.

"How are the clips from today?"

"Excellent. That new kid Jade really stole today's show. I sent one of the interns to find her and do a little background interview."

My pulse speeds up. *I want to do that interview.* But what the hell am I thinking—I never do those. I squelch the impulse. "Sounds good. Keep me posted."

I hang up. I'll go down to the hotel bar and see if there's any action. Female company is never in short supply.

CHAPTER TWO

Jade

I'm not sure what to feel when I get on the bus outside the theater in downtown San Francisco after having thrown away Forbes's handkerchief—I can't stand to not be able to wash it, and there's no way to do that where I'm going. Flashbulbs from the reporters trying to get a shot or a sound bite from those of us who've moved on to the next level of the contest are still burning my eyes as I find a seat. I know I'm exhausted, but don't feel that yet, still high on the thrill of earning the Golden Ticket.

I've run away from home to do this audition.

Well, if it's even running away when you're twenty. But for me, the kid who never goes anywhere, super-responsible, always home when she isn't at the dance studio—this adventure is huge. My disappearance must be causing some freak-out at home.

I've never been so far from Mom before. We Michaels girls grew up in a tiny dot of a town on St. Thomas, in a happy family whose center was the church my parents gave their lives to for twenty years—until my dad died of a stroke when I was fourteen.

God left our family that day, and as far as I can tell, He/She/It hasn't returned.

My oldest sister, Ruby, already married, came to St. Thomas with her husband Rafe and helped Mom pack up the rented house I spent my first fourteen years in. They took eighteen-year-old Pearl, who was doing drugs and boys, back to Boston. I stayed with Mom, traveling to Eureka, California to live with my grandparents.

Until this moment I've lived a quiet, invisible life, a simple loop between home, the ballet studio on Fourth Street where I study dance with my teacher and mentor Jo-Ann Curtola, and school.

After I graduated from high school, the loop only had two stops.

But that's all over now, because this show has been my sole goal for the last three years.

I'd saved enough money from giving lessons to be able to get here and back home, but I didn't want to tell anyone about my attempt to get on *Dance, Dance, Dance* until after the audition, and the cheapest hotel I could find was a two-star on Polk Street. I'll check in, shower, and call home.

The bus, a long, two-sectioned caterpillar, creaks around the corners. Its noise and rocking motion gradually bring me back into my body. I rub hand sanitizer between my hands in thirteen efficient gestures, then gaze out the window to count the utility poles. I nod off briefly, but wake at the driver's call of "Polk Street!" I pick up my gear bag and purse and swing off the bus onto the crowded street.

The hotel's a few blocks west of the bus stop. I've been to San Francisco before, a few trips with Mom and my sister Ruby when she visited with my nephew, but never on my own. Now I find the bustle of the sidewalk and the brisk wind off the Bay bracing, smelling of buses, humanity and the ocean. I circle a clutch of

Chinese women chattering on the corner, a socialite walking a poodle, and a gay couple swinging held hands.

I buy a sandwich at a deli, roast beef with extra mayo as a treat. Carrying my tightly wrapped prize, I climb narrow stairs to the seedy motel, a doorway sandwiched between a head shop and a bar.

I check in with a tattooed clerk sporting so many piercings he could qualify as an earring stand. "Jade Michaels." I plunk my cash down. "I made a reservation."

He smiles. One of his teeth has been pierced too, and a gold star winks at me. "Classy lady." He opens a jingling metal cabinet behind him and extracts a heavy brass key, with a dangling plastic penis attached that designates the room number.

"We don't usually get overnighters," he leers. "Make sure you lock up good."

"Thanks." I head up the rickety stairs, feeling his eyes on my butt. "Time to grow up, Jade Star Michaels," I mutter to myself, refraining from touching the worn metal banister. Once in my shabby room with the door locked, I take my favorite soap out of the bag. It's pale, lavender colored, and I buy it by the twelve-pack at Primm's Victorian Emporium in Eureka.

I can't wait to wash my hands.

The sink has a deep yellow rust stain marking the line of a leak that plunks continually from the tap. I try not to look at it as I run my hands that first sweet time under the cool water.

It takes me exactly thirteen motions to wash my hands, and that's important. Thirteen is bad luck for most people but it's my lucky number. But I'm not going to wash entirely thirteen times today. That's reserved for bad days—and today, for all its challenges, was a very good one.

I get into the shower and luxuriate under the thin flow of water, using my lavender soap all over. My body performed so well today. I appreciate it—everything but the strawberry birthmark in the shape of a heart on my inner thigh. If I could scrub that off, I would. Thank God I didn't get the big breasts both my sisters have—all wrong for dance.

Mom must be worrying about where I am. It's past time for the ordeal of calling her. Out of the shower, I braid my long, wet hair and put on a pair of black sweats. I go back down to the clerk. "Do you have a phone?"

He thumbs down the stairs. "Pay phone on the corner."

"Can I get some change?"

He rolls his eyes. "Good thing I emptied the massage bed this morning."

I hand him a five. He counts out the quarters, and I trot down the steps outside past the noisy bar next to the place. At the pay phone, I feed in quarters and dial the familiar number of home.

I'm surprised when it rings the requisite five times before dumping into the answering machine. Somehow I'd expected Mom to be home, waiting for my call—but maybe this isn't as big a deal as I'd thought.

"Hey, Mom. Just wanted to let you know that I'm in San Francisco. I didn't want to tell you anything until I found out what happened, but I auditioned for that TV show we like—you know, *Dance, Dance, Dance*? Well, I got on to the next level! I'm going to LA, all expenses paid." I blew out a breath, wondering what else there was to say. "Sorry if I worried you, but this was something I just had to do myself. And you can keep an eye on the show and see how I do." I pause again, thinking of Mom's strongly boned face, her hazel eyes surrounded by care lines that deepened after Dad died. "Don't worry, I'll be fine. I'll call again in a couple of days." I hang up and turn away from the phone, only to feel a tug on my arm.

Someone's trying to grab my purse! I clutch my arm tighter to my side. "Hey! Let go!"

I'm wrestling a teenaged kid. Fortunately, he's around my size.

"Let go, bitch, or I'll cut you," he yells, tugging at my strap with one hand and brandishing a pocketknife with the other.

"No! You let go!" I yell back. "Help! He's stealing my purse!"

A passerby shoves the kid, who staggers comically before falling off the curb into the culvert. He scrambles to his feet and takes off.

I hug my bag close, feeling adrenaline wash over me.

Everything I have is in this purse—my ID, my Golden Ticket, the few dollars I have to my name—everything.

"Hey miss, you okay?" The guy who knocked the purse snatcher off me pats my shoulder. He's a head or so taller, and handsome in a golden-skinned way that reminds me of some of the men of my home island of St. Thomas, descended from a mix of races.

"Thanks so much. I'm fine. Oh, God. That was close."

"He was just a kid."

"He would still have taken everything I have." I shiver at the thought.

Warm brown eyes crinkle at the corners. "I know the feeling. Hey—didn't I see you at the audition?"

I swivel to face him fully. "You saw me at the audition?"

"You were hard to miss." He grins, extends a hand. "Alex Rodriguez. Happy I'm a dude so I don't have to compete against you in the contest." Two winners are chosen in *Dance, Dance, Dance*—a male and a female. I look him over as I shake his hand briefly—it's warm, dry and strong. I resist the urge to reach into my purse for the hand sanitizer.

"Are you staying around here?" I gesture to the seedy area surrounding us, where neon signs for bars and massage parlors glow in the lengthening shadows.

"That fleabag." He gestures to my motel. "Surprised they didn't charge me by the hour."

"I had the same thought."

"Well—you hungry? We could grab a bite."

I mentally tick through my choices. My belly is gnawing and all my energy reserves were used up during the tryout—but do I have enough money?

"My treat." Alex sees my hesitation. He extends an elbow in a courtly-gentleman way. "And in case you think I'm hitting on you—I'm gay." He winks. "No ulterior motives."

I feel my cheeks heat. Ruby, my oldest sister and a sharp lawyer, always said I have a ridiculously easy face to read. "I'd love to get something to eat. But let me pick up the tip, at least."

"It's a deal."

I set my hand lightly in the crook of his elbow, wishing I didn't have to touch him—but I have to get over that. The dancing is all couples on the show.

"We'll probably have to dance together at least once in the next few weeks," Alex says, as if reading my mind. "So we might as well get to know each other. Where are you from?"

"Eureka, California." We navigate around a wino weaving toward us, reeking of booze and vomit.

"Where?"

"Ass end of California. Logging town almost on the border of Oregon," I say. "But St. Thomas before that. You?"

"Oh, St. Thomas!" Alex rolls his eyes to heaven and shudders in mock ecstasy. "Is it as beautiful as they say?"

"Probably more so." A memory of crystalline Magens Bay directly across the street from our modest plantation house, with its deep porch and shady roof, swamps me momentarily with homesickness. We weren't rich, but we were happy there—until Dad died, and everything changed. On the other hand, I never would have learned to dance in St. Thomas—and dancing is the only thing that really makes me happy. "You never answered where you're from."

"Right here. My family lives in the East Bay." He gestures with a hand toward the urban sprawl across the Bay, visible as we reach a downward slope in the steep street.

"So, where are you taking me?" I'm glad of the heavy sweats I put on as a chill wind blasts up the hill, swirling leaves and bits of trash around my legs.

"Little place I know. I've got a lot of friends in the city and one of the things they do well in San Francisco is food." He steers me around a newspaper kiosk. "But it's a few blocks away, so you can use the walk to tell me about yourself."

"Not much to tell." I let go of his arm.

"Yes, there is. There's a story behind a girl that got started dancing at fourteen and still developed crazy moves." Alex gets in front of me, talking as he walks backward. "Let me know if I knock any old ladies or hot dudes off the sidewalk."

I laugh and shake my head. "Okay. My dad died, which is why we had to leave St. Thomas. We moved to my mom's parents' house in Eureka. I was super miserable." I can hardly bear to remember how miserable, everything known and familiar gone, just me and Mom in the creaky old Victorian. Getting used to the cold, chilly rain that was one of Eureka's defining characteristics alone was difficult. "Mom put me in dance lessons because..." I wasn't going to tell him about my OCD, how my nonstop cleaning, counting, and rituals had driven Mom to send me somewhere that would 'get me out of my head.' "I needed something physical to do."

"But how'd you master all those styles?"

"Watching music videos on MTV while the adults were out of the house."

"Yes!" Alex grins big and holds his hand up for a high five.

"Watch out!" I cry, but it's too late—he trips, arms wind milling, and crashes into a hip-looking young couple.

"Sorry!" he exclaims. I take his arm and turn him around.

"Eyes on the road, buddy. Now tell me about you, and why you're trying out for this crazy dance thing."

"Youngest of five, so Mom and Pops pretty much let me do whatever I want. We're from Puerto Rico originally, but I was born here, and I've been dancing since I was this high." He makes a gesture near his knees. "I never was drawn to one particular style, but ended up doing more breakdancing than anything else since that's what guys do on the street in the East Bay."

"Show me some moves," I say. "I want to see what I'm going to be dealing with. That is—if you made it to the next round?"

"I did. And to celebrate, I'll show you this." He whips a Walkman out of a roomy pocket and plugs in a tiny speaker, then sets it on the sidewalk. "Might as well see what we can get," he says with a twinkle, and throws down his Chicago Bulls ball cap.

I laugh as the Bee Gees' *Stayin' Alive* bursts out of the small, surprisingly powerful speaker. Alex busts into a spin, dropping to do some ground work, arching up and exiting in a flip. I'm clapping with the beat, smiling, and a crowd gathers, applauding at Alex's uninhibited, fearless breaking. Coins rattle into the ball cap, then a few bills, and then Alex grabs me by the hand as *Stayin' Alive* gives way to *Play that Funky Music*.

I'm still clutching my purse, but with a grin he snatches it from me, and picking up on the playful mime, I act horrified until he puts it under the cap filled with money. I'm laughing as he takes my hand and swivels his hips like they're a gyroscope. Facing him, I match his rock step, letting my hips out to play too, and he swirls me into a cha-cha.

Fortunately, this is one ballroom dance I took lessons for, and the seventies song is surprisingly perfect for cha-cha. We circle around my purse and the increasingly full ball cap and get down and funky, riffing off each other's moves as he plays ardent pursuer and I, shy ingénue.

Alex can dance, that's for sure, and he knows how to lead and has some darned sexy moves. I can feel a magnetic chemistry building between us, and he sure doesn't seem gay in the moment as he dips me, twirls me, and spins me out and in, all to the unlikeliest song.

Our impromptu performance continues to be a crowd-pleaser. When the song ends, we get a round of applause and dollar bills flutter like confetti as Alex runs around making a comedy out of capturing the money and coins, tossing them in the air to catch them behind his back, juggling them, stuffing them into his pockets and around his belt like a stripper.

I retrieve my purse and watch, grinning, as he pretends to find a quarter behind a kid's ear and then presses it into the child's hand. "Keep the change," he says magnanimously, and returns to take my arm.

We skip down the sidewalk, because Alex makes me. "Are you sure you're gay?" I say as we reach a little storefront restaurant with CHOW on the window in gold letters.

He laughs. "Oh honey. I'm whatever I need to be on the dance floor." He pushes open the door of the restaurant with a showy bow. A bell tinkles overhead, and good smells surround us. "This is one of the best restaurants in the city. Prepare to be amazed."

"All right." My cheeks hot from exertion, my hair unraveling from my braid, I'm happier right now than I remember being... maybe ever? But in just the span of an hour, Alex has brought more fun into my life than I've had in years.

Ruby's the achiever, Pearl's the rebel—and I'm the introvert with OCD. *But not when I'm dancing.* When I'm dancing, I'm just me. The best part of me. I never think of my rituals when I'm dancing, and the need to count things is a strength—I learn steps quickly.

But thinking about my OCD makes me remember all the touching I've been doing, and I need to wash my hands.

"Where's the restroom?"

He points to it. "Want me to order you a beer? We have plenty of loot to pay for dinner."

"Oh no. I'm not legal yet." I stand up from the table, clutching my purse.

"You aren't serious," he bulges his eyes comically. "Refusing alcohol after a day like today? You can pass for twenty-one. I'm getting you a beer."

"But even if I passed for twenty-one, as you say, I don't drink. Too many calories."

"Bet you're a virgin too."

My cheeks get hotter. "None of your business." I march off to hear his low, teasing whistle behind me.

"Sassy bugger," I say to my reflection. "I'm not discussing my sex life—or lack of it—with someone I met an hour ago."

Of course I'm a frickin' virgin. I can hardly stand to touch anyone's hand, let alone their...

I undo my braid and let my hair down, a river of dark auburn ripples that brush the top of my waist, and fluff it out. Mom's hair, when she was younger. I splash water on my face to cool down my red cheeks, and wash my hands. Two pumps of soap, thirteen quick passes through the water, one paper towel thoroughly used, even under my nails.

People don't know how really stressful OCD can be.

Alex whistles again, in a different way, as I return to the table. There's a beer in front of my place setting, deep amber with a head of foam on it an inch deep. I sit down and give him a quelling glance, to which he winks. "You danced enough today to earn one beer. Or are you a virgin with alcohol too?" he says.

"Stop teasing me." I slurp at the foam. It's tangy, yeasty, and not entirely horrible. "We're going to have problems if you keep teasing me."

"But you blush," Alex says, smacking his lips loudly over his beer. "And you don't know how rare that is—irresistible, too. Here's your cut of tonight's loot." He pushes a pile of coins and bills over to me.

"No, no. You did all that," I protest, and push the pile back.

"C'mon. There's always more tomorrow." He pushes the money back to me again. "Let's do some pop and lock tomorrow. That's always a good haul. The crowds love it."

"Aren't we going to LA tomorrow?" I give in and pour the cash off the bread plate he'd set it on into my purse. I really do need it, after all.

"Not till later. How do you think I'm paying for all this?" Alex makes an expansive gesture, grinning. He has a dimple and perfect white teeth. The girls are going to love him on the show, more fool they.

"You're the friend I've always wanted and never had," I say fervently, as a plate of pasta with two fist-sized meatballs swimming in red sauce and Parmesan cheese arrives. I'm lightheaded with hunger. "I bet you can even give me clothing advice."

"A complete overhaul is what you need, if those awful sweats are any indication. And wait until I can get my hands on your hair." Alex eyes the disordered tresses blanketing my shoulders. "I'm a hairdresser when I'm not dancing. Yeah, I'm the friend you've always needed."

I moan, biting into my pasta and meatball. "Oh, sweet baby. This is the best thing I've ever eaten."

"You haven't seen me really dance yet." Alex points his fork at me. "That's the best thing in the world. Except for you, maybe, but the crowd will decide that."

I kick him under the table, and he laughs.

CHAPTER THREE

Brandon

THERE'S A LOT TO DO to move *Dance, Dance, Dance* from the tryout phase to the big LA film studio where we are putting together the rest of the show, but even though I've got a hundred things on my mind and clipboard, I flag down one of my assistants. "I want to run that mini-interview with Jade Michaels. Where's the footage on that?"

"Who, Boss?" The kid looks cross-eyed with stress so I enunciate very slowly and clearly.

"Jade Michaels. Green eyes. Auburn hair. About this high." I gesture to my collarbone. "Rocked the audition so hard she danced an entire song and never got beeped off the stage."

"Oh yeah." The kid, whose ID reads Clay, looks down at his clipboard. I dimly remember he's an intern from UCLA, and thus his ass is mine without pay for the next six months. "Number 260. I don't see a checkbox by her name... looks like no one did the interview."

I shouldn't be so pissed, but I am. "Clay from UCLA. Are you frickin' kidding me? Jade spiked viewer interest like crazy."

My voice rises. "Her interview segment was supposed to get done yesterday. Who screwed up?"

"Sorry, Boss. I don't know. I'll find out for you." The little cockroach scuttles off with his head down.

Son of a... I want that footage, and finding out who screwed up isn't going to get it for me. "Somebody find Jade Michaels!" I bellow. "I want that interview!"

"Yeah, Boss, on it," another one of the interns, Tad from Yale, quavers. "I have an address of a motel in the Tenderloin."

"You know, when you want things done right, sometimes you just have to do them yourself," I snarl, and hand off my clipboard to Tad from Yale. "Get going on the things on this list, and if you screw up you're gone from the show. I need a cameraman!"

I head for the bright green exit sign. Stomping as I go feels good. Gotta keep these people on their toes.

"You need to get laid," Stu says as he gets into the cab with me after stowing his bulky camera equipment in the trunk. He's the only cameraman brave enough to follow me out. "You're way too wound up."

"When we get to LA, maybe. Glad this part is over." I didn't follow through with any of the opportunities in stilettos at the hotel bar last night. Right now, I can't even say why I'm so pissed off that Jade's interview didn't get done—or why I want to do it myself. I don't want to think too much about it, quite frankly. I sit back against the lumpy upholstery and massage my temples as the cab moves out. "What I really need is more coffee."

"It's a dance show, not frickin' rocket science. Why do we have to do this interview right now? We can catch her in LA." Stu's been my friend since college and working the show since it started. He knows me better than my own mother does—which wouldn't be hard, come to think of it. He's a skinny guy who dresses Goth and has ear gauges I'm always tempted to pull. Today he's wearing eyeliner and three days' worth of beard.

"You look like a freak. Dress professional when you come to work," I snap.

"What? Like you?" He gestures to the running clothes I put on in the dark of my room before I jogged from the Fairmont to the studio. "Bitch all you want. I'm not your employee."

Stu loves to remind me he's an independent contractor whenever it suits him.

We drive in grumpy silence to Jade's motel. It's a fleabag in the worst part of San Francisco. Getting out of the cab, I spot a discarded syringe caught in a crack in the sidewalk. A dark brown sundae-like pile of dog crap near the curb smells suspiciously like human excrement. There's a fritzing neon beer sign on one side and a head shop on the other. The motel's creaky sign flashes VACANCY.

"Get a shot of this, Stu. Girl obviously doesn't have a lot." I feel anger stir in my chest. I know this family. Jade's older sister Ruby is loaded, a lawyer married to some Boston blueblood millionaire, and Pearl is a highly paid supermodel, for crying out loud. "What the hell is she doing in a place like this?" I mutter aloud.

Stu gets his gear going and begins filming, panning around the filthy street and then walking slowly to the entrance, the stabilizer mount on his shoulder keeping the camera from jiggling.

Why isn't the supposedly loving Michaels family doing anything to support their little sister? This place is downright dangerous. I'm even more pissed now that we got here. I pace up and down the sidewalk. No one will meet my eye, and I realize I'm looking for her.

"Get ahead of me, Brandon. I can get the whole seedy picture as you walk up those stairs," Stu says, his camera ready. "Make sure to flex your ass. The chicks will love that in those tight nylon pants you're wearing."

"Screw you." But I do flex a little, walking up the stairs. Can't hurt to add a little something to the dailies, since I didn't dress right for being on camera.

The desk clerk is so tatted up his features are hard to make out. His eyes slide around in the gift wrap of his face like shiny brown olives.

"Jade Michaels. What room is she in?" I throw down a twenty on the counter. Stu has his camera on the guy, and the man makes a waving gesture to get it away. "I can't give out confidential information on our guests." But his eyes dart down to the twenty. I hold up my hand for Stu to turn the camera off—we got the atmosphere shot, anyway.

I throw another twenty down on top of the first. "Memory getting any better?"

"Matter of fact it is. The girl checked out already." The weasel grabs my money so fast I can't get it back. My arms are twitching with the need to hit him as I stare him down.

"Let's get another shot outside for filler," Stu says in the low voice people use for calming babies and old people.

Outside on the curb, I head downhill, not sure why. I just need to move, and Stu needs to grab background clips that can be interspersed with Jade's interview. My brain is buzzing with questions for her—questions I realize aren't right for her on-camera interview. Questions that have to do with me knowing her family, because I dated her sister—a sister she clearly didn't want to discuss. "We're not close," Jade had said, and that sweet, lush, exactly-like-Pearl mouth closed, an expression on it like sucking an old penny.

I hear music. A little tinny and hollow, but loud enough to tickle the ears and tantalize—and it's *disco*.

Who the hell plays disco on the street in San Francisco?

I reach the corner and look further downhill. Halfway down the next block, in front of a busy coffee shop, I see a crowd gathered around two dancers doing pop and lock. One of them is Jade.

I recognize her immediately as a gleam of sunlight hits her hair. What color is that? Is it red? Or like, a deep mahogany? Reminds me of my mom's good dining room table—the one we never sit at except for what I call Melissa's "state dinners," when she's entertaining potential clients.

Jade is dancing with that Puerto Rican kid with the loose hips. Man, the dude can move. He's like a robotic Gumby.

"Stu!" I bellow. "Get your camera over here!" I set off down the sidewalk and hear him running to catch up. Stu sticks to my back as I hit the edge of the crowd watching our two contestants work the sidewalk.

"Get the shot. Whatever you do, get this shot," I growl, pushing rudely through the crowd and making a way for the cameraman. We reach the edge and Stu gets the camera on the two of them, who appear oblivious to us and everyone watching.

They're playing a game of follow-and-lead to the beat of *Hot Stuff* by Donna Summer, a totally incongruous clash of styles that weirdly works. First, the kid, whose first name I mentally dredge up as Alex, does a mime-in-the-box and then an ab ripple. Jade, across from him, repeats it and then does her riff: a shoulder ripple that ends in a triangle shape with her arms and a little Egyptian head-and-neck funky chicken.

Alex imitates her perfectly.

The crowd applauds. Coins rattle and bills rustle into a Chicago Bulls hat set on the sidewalk next to a Walkman and speaker combo.

The song ends as they both bust out with some freestyle breaking. I can't believe the crispness and aggression of Jade's moves. She's wearing ballet gear, too, pink tights and leotard, one of those filmy wrap skirts that teases the imagination, and her hair is braided around her head in a crown like she was going out for

Swan Lake. The contrast makes her unforgettable. Alex, shirtless, bronzed, and wearing baggy MC Hammer pants, provides a great foil.

These two are serious contenders. I can feel a grin stretching my cheeks. Some damn fine moves there, and the fact that they're both eye candy doesn't hurt their chances. The song ends, the money rains down, and Stu is grinning from ear to ear, pasted to his viewfinder.

"Yeah, Boss," he says out of the side of his mouth. "I got the shot. And it's gold."

Jade

Alex is doing his stripper-picking-up-bills imitation as I pose like a marionette with its strings cut, one elbow up and swinging, the rest of me dangling limp. My eyes stay down, in character, but out of my peripheral vision I track a TV camera on us, held by a man that looks like a strip of black licorice.

There's someone beside him. One of the producers. My eyes track up his body slowly—well-turned legs in tight gray Adidas running pants. Trim hips, big hands resting on them. A matching nylon mesh-paneled running shirt with short sleeves that hugs a body too thickly muscular to be a dancer's. Wide, tanned neck. Square jaw. Short blond hair. Hazel eyes, pinned on mine.

Brandon Forbes. The show producer that helped me off the stage at my audition.

The guy who used to date Pearl. I cut my eyes back down. The heat in his eyes as he looks at me is Pearl's leftovers. And I won't be Pearl's leftovers in any way, shape, or form.

I unwind fluidly and stand upright. I give a plié and curtsy to the applauding crowd as Alex sweeps a bow beside me like a shirtless genie, and we finish our act.

The crowd disperses and Forbes and the cameraman approach.

"That motel is no place for you," are the first words out of Forbes's mouth as he looms over me.

I tip my head to glare at him. "I didn't see a voucher for anything better in the packet you gave me, thank you very much."

That shuts him up.

Alex inserts himself between us with an extended hand. "Hey, Mr. Forbes. I recognize you from the show—you're the main producer, right? Dare I hope you were filming us for one of those mini-interviews you guys do?"

"Yes." Forbes finally stops glaring at me and turns to Alex. "We came looking for Miss Michaels here, and were lucky enough to catch your lucrative performance." His brows snap back down over those golden-green eyes as he swivels back to me. "If you needed money all you needed to do was ask," he growls at me.

"Why? Because you dated my sister?" I flare back at him. "I'm doing this on my own time and dime, not that it's any of your damn business."

I never snap at people like that. "Miss Mouse" is what I'm called at the studio. I can be so quiet people forget I'm in the room.

"Ahem," Alex interjects with his charming grin. "Ms. Michaels is a little giddy from her exertions. She's thrilled with the opportunity of this interview and the support of *Dance, Dance, Dance*. In fact, she graciously accepts your offer of better lodgings, since what you see here is pretty much the kind of place we planned to get in LA." Alex slings an arm, unpleasantly hot and sweaty, over my shoulders. "We're roommates."

I think Forbes is going to blow a gasket at that, but he nods. "Fine. I'll put you two on an expense account. We can't have our contestants getting mugged. Let's get back to the studio and shoot your interview before we have to clear out and leave for LA."

He spins and takes off, walking at a speed that makes the rest of us jog to keep up. Alex helps the poor cameraman with his heavy gear. I keep my eyes on Forbes as he stalks up the hill, scanning for a cab and waving one down.

He holds the door for me and I scramble past him to enter, my backpack and purse, which we'd been using to prop up the ball cap, clutched close. He ends up sitting next to me with Alex on the other side of him and the cameraman up front with the cabbie.

I plaster myself against the door but Forbes is wedged against me. His whole body is large and hot and most of it's touching me: his shoulder against mine, his bulky arm against my side, our thighs aligned.

I'm suffocating. All this touching, and in a confined space. I turn my head and plaster my face against the cool, curved glass of the window, my gaze on the passing buildings. I count the streetlights to calm the racing heart and sweating palms brought on by being crowded against him. *One. Two. Three. Four. Five. Six. Seven...*

The counting calms me and I breathe a little easier once I reach lucky thirteen. I begin over again with one.

"You two were good." Forbes's voice is a warm pleasant baritone and I can feel it vibrate through his shoulder. He sounds calmer, too, and like he's trying to be nice, but his voice interrupts my counting and I have to start again, moving my lips silently.

"Thanks. I'm from the East Bay and earn some money on the weekend street dancing," Alex says. "Turns out this girl has a few moves too, and isn't too stuck up to partner with me."

I struggle to keep counting but have to mutter the numbers aloud to keep track. "Seven, eight..." I press the button to roll down the window repeatedly, but nothing happens. The driver must have it locked.

"What are you doing?" Forbes asks, ignoring Alex. I wish he would leave me alone.

"Nothing." I press my forehead into the window. Hard. The pressure kind of helps and I start counting again.

"Do you want the window down?" His breath tickles the loose strands of my hair around my ear and I shiver.

"Yes."

"Driver! Put the left rear window down," he barks, so loudly that I jump.

The cabbie turns his head. "You got it."

The window rolls down and a rush of cool air flows over me in blessed relief. I hang my head out the window like a panting golden retriever. "Thanks. I don't like small spaces," I say over my shoulder.

Forbes doesn't reply. His gaze is intent, and his face is too close, even with the open space the taxi's window has created. There are crinkles beside his remarkable hazel eyes, and a shadow of beard on his jaw, and his mouth is a contrast of cushiony lips and hard angles.

I wonder how much older than me he is. He seems a couple of years older than Pearl, but not too much older. Maybe six or seven years older than me?

Just right.

Just right for what?

Rattled, I snap my head around and start counting again.

Mercifully, we reach the studio within another couple of blocks and the minute the taxi stops, I scramble out of the back seat. I hurry into the studio building without waiting for the others and head straight for the bathroom.

I lock the door and wash my hands thirteen times.

It works. By the end of thirteen, I'm ready to look at the parts of me that touched him and see if any need to be washed. It's okay though. I was covered—tights on me, pants on him. Our shoulders were covered.

Still, somehow I'm left with a sense of his body imprinted on mine. I'm so unsettled by it. I want to shower just so I can erase the feeling.

There's no shower here. I will just have to get used to this, and a lot more touching in the days ahead.

I brace myself on the sink and count thirteen slow breaths, and slowly my heart rate settles.

A knock at the door spikes it again.

"Jade?" Alex's voice sounds worried. "Mr. Forbes wants to interview us. You okay in there?"

"Sure, of course. Just freshening up. I'll be there in a minute." I dig in my bag and put on some pale rose lipstick, blusher, and a little kohl eyeliner and mascara. Everyone says the camera bleaches you out, and I need all the help I can get.

CHAPTER FOUR

Brandon

JADE'S TAKING FOREVER IN THE bathroom as Stu and I set up a drape in the corner of the studio. Most of our stuff has been packed up already. Rows of Pelican cases filled with sound and camera equipment are waiting to be loaded up, piles of cord wrapped into bundles stacked beside them. We rented this filming area furnished and have our own fully equipped studio down in LA, so as long as this place is packed up as good as we found it, there's not much more to do than pull together our personal items and get on the plane.

But I want that footage first.

Stu plugs in a couple of spots and hangs a reflection umbrella.

I put on a new, pressed shirt and pale green tie that the stylist hands me, but keep my running pants on. They won't show in the shot.

Jade's still not out of the damn bathroom, so I interview Alex first.

The kid's confident, funny, and self-deprecating, and I can tell by Stu's expression of semi-rapture that the camera loves him.

Alex's gayness also becomes abundantly clear, illustrated by feminine gesturing and a flirtatious manner.

I shouldn't be so relieved. I have no reason to give two shits about his orientation, but I didn't like the way he threw an arm over Jade and so confidently claimed her as his 'roommate.'

Jade finally comes up beside Stu, who has his camera on a tripod now that we're in a stable location. I wrap up the interview. "So glad you could join us for *Dance, Dance, Dance*, Alex. After what we saw on the street, I'm sure you're going to be a strong competitor for male Dancer of the Year."

"Thank you." Alex hops off the stool and executes a showy pirouette ending with a bow. "I dance to win."

"Sounds like a bumper sticker."

"Make it so," he intones, in exactly the tone of Patrick Stewart on the *Star Trek* show, and I laugh and make the wrap motion. The kid's really charming.

I glance down at my notes, and review the questions I'm going to ask Jade.

She'd really seemed on the verge of a panic attack in the cab —and that murmuring she was doing sure sounded like counting. She seemed better after the window went down, but still couldn't get out of the cab fast enough—almost like she was fleeing from me, like touching me freaked her out.

Jade's a spooky little thing. Very different from bright Ruby and bold Pearl. She's her own person, and clearly doing this on her own "time and dime," as she put it.

Good for her.

I look up at last. Jade's sitting on the chair we set up, her eyes downcast. The spotlight on the crown of her hair shows that it's definitely brown—but with deep red in it, like cherry wood with a good grain. Her hands are folded primly in her lap. The pale pink of her long sleeve leotard, tights, and flimsy swish of a skirt is just a shade pinker than her skin. She has small, high breasts and a tiny waist bisected by a black ribbon. Her legs, crossed at the ankle, are long, slender, and perfect.

I'd like to see her naked on a pure white bed, wearing nothing but her hair and that black ribbon around her waist.

I shake my head to get rid of the intrusive thought and clear my throat. "Welcome to *Dance, Dance, Dance,* Jade. I'm Brandon Forbes, producer of the show."

"Thanks. I'm honored to be here." Jade's voice is low. I make a hand gesture for the team to jack up her mic.

"We were really impressed with your audition, and again with the surprise street performance we caught you and Alex doing. Why don't you tell us a little about yourself and what brings you here to the competition?"

"Sure." Jade folds one of her legs and hooks her interlaced fingers around it, heel in its ballet slipper resting on one of the stool's slats. "I'm from Eureka, California..." She recites facts woodenly, as if reading from a teleprompter. The charisma that animated her dancing has vanished—she looks like any young, naive contestant with a rehearsed speech.

Boring as hell.

I need to provoke the life I've seen in her. "Something our audience may not know is that you're the sister of a supermodel that we all know and love: Pearl. She's so internationally famous that she goes by just her first name! Tell us, what's it like to be the kid sister of a woman that's known as one of the seven most beautiful women in the world?"

I know I went too far with that last sentence as the delicate color in Jade's face drains away, leaving red patches on her cheeks. Her eyes widen, large and glittery-hard as emeralds. Clearly, she's forgotten she's on national TV as she says, "It sucks. In fact, it couldn't be worse. And you better not have allowed me on this show because you're still hung up on her, Brandon Forbes, because if so, I'm out that door."

We lock eyes. I feel heat on my neck—as if I'd do something like that! More like I'd cut her because she was related to Pearl.

I let a long beat pass by—there will be a space in the video where I can have that segment cut from the interview. Stu doesn't need to be told this part won't be going into the show. I pick up the thread again, this time with a smile that I hope is gentle and understanding.

"Let's both just take a breath and try that again." Another beat. Jade's green eyes are still huge and diamond-hard, but I press on. "Something the audience might not know is that you're Pearl's little sister—yes, the international supermodel so famous she only goes by her first name. Tell us a little about the talent that runs in your family."

Color surges back into her face. Jade licks her lips, a flicker of her pink tongue. Her eyes glance to the left as she thinks of how to answer.

Damn, I could watch that expressive face all day. Her charisma is back, that ineffable something that the camera eats up and translates into addicting.

"I love both of my amazing sisters. Ruby is a lawyer. Married with a little boy. She lives in Boston and I get to see her a couple of times a year. She's always encouraged me in my dancing and helped pay for my lessons, since finances have been hard since our dad died. And Pearl. Pearl is just an inspiration by being who she is." Jade's smile is wide and fake.

She and Pearl clearly don't get along. I'm tempted to probe but I want to keep the good juju going for the cameras—the last thing I want is for her to storm off the show.

"You began dancing at fourteen, which as I'm sure you're aware, is late for a professional career in dance. Tell us more about how it happened that way."

"My dad died, is how it happened." Sadness fills her voice and her sweet, pouty mouth droops. Her lashes cast spiky shadows on her cheeks in the harsh spotlight. I flick my eyes to Stu. He knows I'm looking and gives a thumbs up, zooming in to capture her emotion. We're getting good stuff now.

"We had to leave St. Thomas and move back to the United States." She tells how hard it was for her mother to keep up the vacation rental business her parents ran without her father's help, and how they moved back to Eureka where the grandparents lived. Her mother began a new business, managing rentals for the college students at Humboldt State. It was hard for her to make ends meet, and older sister Ruby stepped in to pay for lessons, camps, and outfits for Jade's dancing. "Ruby could see how dancing helped me. I had some—emotional problems after we got to Eureka."

"Tell us about those." I press forward, though I can see she didn't want to let that slip.

"And give away all my secrets in the first interview?" Jade ducks her head and dimples at me. That demure, flirty look goes straight to my groin. I can feel the erection I've been fighting ever since I sat next to her in the taxi tenting the front of those damn nylon running pants, and I'm glad of the table that blocks any view from the waist down.

I laugh politely. "I'm sure we'll have more chances to get to know you, Miss Michaels—you're going to go far in this contest if your audition is anything to go by."

"I hope so. Thanks so much for the chance." Jade addresses this comment directly to the camera. Stu zooms in on her rose-leaf cheeks, flashing eyes, and dewy smile.

"That's a wrap," I say, and he shuts off the camera.

Jade slides off the stool without making eye contact with me, and bounds like a springbok to the bathroom again.

She's obviously got issues. The last thing I need is to get involved with another Michaels girl—but another part of me still hasn't gotten the memo.

CHAPTER FIVE

Jade

THE ONLY TIME I'VE EVER been to LA was when I was
sixteen and Pearl had a fashion show with the other Big Six
supermodels. She sent Mom tickets, and Mom wouldn't take no
for an answer on me going. We flew into the massive maze that
was LAX and took a taxi to the hotel where the fashion show was
being held—and then we spent the next forty-eight hours indoors.
I only remember the show as a blur of glossy, passing bodies,
sparkling fabrics, and pulsing music. At the awful after-party, I
collected pitying glances: Pearl's awkward little wallflower sister,
sitting in the corner, hiding behind thick glasses.

I didn't get contacts until I was eighteen, mostly because of
my germ phobia. How could I put those bacteria-laden plastic
discs in my eyes? But after that LA party, I decided I had to get
over the problem enough to wear contacts. My glasses were just
too thick for me to keep wearing while dancing, for one thing.

But the upshot was, I had little idea what LA was like. It felt
like I'd never been there before at all, when the plane came down
the same afternoon as my uncomfortable interview with Brandon

Forbes. The built-up concrete sprawl of the city seemed like its own kind of Amazonian jungle: rivers of cars, tangles of wires, and stands of buildings so thick they blocked out the sun.

"We're not in Kansas anymore," I comment to Alex as we get into a taxi for the hotel where the show is lodging contestants.

He shrugs. "I've been down here a bunch of times to do dance battles. It's where the work is. If you want to dance, better get used to it. This, or New York, is the heart of dance in this country."

Looking out the window, I feel my breath shrivel a little in my chest. I can't see anything but cars, asphalt, and graffiti.

I missed the cool green redwoods around Eureka with a sudden fierceness. Maybe I was a country girl at heart—but I'd chosen work that called for the city.

The Marriott housing us is an older one, right next to the massive studio building where the show will be filmed. Looking at that steel structure, gray and drab in the low afternoon light, my pulse picks up.

This is so amazing—and it's happening to unlucky *me*.

And it has nothing to do with Pearl.

At least I hope not. I frown, remembering Forbes's questions. What a jerk. Like I couldn't tell he was trying to get a rise out of me—and of course, he succeeded. At least I'd been able to respond appropriately to the second question he posed, and end on a cutesy note that would hopefully play to the audience.

The taxi dumps us off at the curb in front of the Marriott. I immediately shrug out of the wool pea coat I donned in San Francisco—the sun might be low here, but it's a full ten degrees warmer.

"Still up for being roommates?" I ask Alex.

"I don't know if they'll let us share," Alex is wound tight, bright and alert as a parakeet in a gold satin warm-up jacket and teal pants with black Converse sneakers. The lobby is filled with knots of talking young people. Their clothing and bodies mark them as fellow competitors. I pull out a squirt bottle of hand sanitizer and rub my hands together thirteen times as Alex sees someone he knows and goes off. I head straight for the check-in counter.

"Reservation for Jade Michaels. I'm with the *Dance, Dance, Dance* show." I extract the voucher in my Golden Ticket envelope. "Can I room with my friend, Alex Rodriguez?"

The clerk types rapidly. Her eyebrows rise into a fringe of curled, dyed-red bangs. "You have an upgrade on your room to a two-room suite, authorized by the show's producers. Alex Rodriguez has one room, you the other."

So Forbes followed through. I have to admit, I'm shocked. I look around for Alex and wave him over to tell him the news.

"He's got the hots for you." Alex throws an arm over me as he makes a kissing motion with his lips.

"Ugh, no! My sister's sloppy seconds!" I realize, with a stab of unexpected pain, that I really wish it was me he liked—but how could that ever be? Pearl eclipses me in every way. "He's still hung up on my sister Pearl. You know, the supermodel? They dated."

"Holy shit! Pearl? *The* Pearl? She's your sister?" Alex does a good imitation of the kid in *Home Alone*, his mouth and eyes wide in a comical scream. "And Forbes got his hands on that? Well, yeah. Is he hoping to get her back or something? Cuz I heard she was married—to like, some huge special ops guy built like a tank."

"She's married, all right. Very married." I actually like Magnus, her husband. He's a good guy, if a little scary. And Pearl's been nice to me for years now—those old bullying days were ages ago, when Dad was alive and she was experimenting with drugs. Now she's just internationally famous as one of the world's seven most beautiful women. Her attempts to "help" pitiful me by giving me makeup tips and such have just made me feel worse.

Pearl and I avoid each other now. She can't help being who she is, and she does what she does to me just by being who she is.

I almost can't bear it that Brandon Forbes is so attractive, and in charge of the show, and even has a nice side. I'd be daydreaming about him right now, worse even than my Baryshnikov fantasies, if he weren't Pearl's ex. With her for comparison, though, there's no way he'll see me as anything but Pearl's weird little sister who spends a lot of time in the bathroom.

"Forbes doesn't seem like he comes in second at anything, and if I thought there was a chance in hell he swung my direction, I'd take a bite of that," Alex goes on. "But whatever. I'm glad I'm along for *your* ride, as far as that elevator takes me."

The elevator, it turns out, takes us to the penthouse floor at the top of the building.

LA can look beautiful when the sun's going down. The lights come on like a million scattered stars spread in a glittering blanket. Sitting in a comfy chair, sipping on a tiny bottle of vodka from the hotel bar with a good friend, I toast to the first day of the rest of my life.

Brandon

Everything's in place for the show, and that means the set is total chaos. We have two hundred contestants, and the judges' unenviable task is to cut the herd by at least fifty a day until we have our final top twenty couples. They cull the herd by putting them into big groups and teaching some complicated routine with a couple of dance instructors. The judges walk around and through them, cutting the ones that aren't catching on fast enough, that crowd others, that can't pick up on a new style, or that just look shitty for whatever reason.

A steady flow of emotionally wrecked young men and women flow out through the doors that admitted them this same optimistic morning.

My job is to oversee everything and be about ten steps ahead of everyone else. I'm glad of the glassed-in viewing office this film studio features. I can work on my shit from the sanity of my quiet desk and phone, and still have a look down at the carnage whenever it suits me.

I've kept the area in front of the glass window clear so I can pace back and forth and talk on the cordless phone. I'm haggling with one of the studio heads about next season when I spot Jade in the crowd below.

She's in what I'm coming to think of as her "trademark" outfit, that pale pink ballet rig, and this time her hair is in a French braid that comes to the middle of her back. I bet her hair almost touches her waist when it's down. I've never seen it down.

She's in one of the big groups, learning a ballroom step with interchanging partners. My voice trails off as I see one of the judges, unmistakable in one of the bright yellow *Dance, Dance, Dance* logo T-shirts we issued them, advancing toward her.

"Holy shit, is she getting cut?" My hands go sweaty. It never occurred to me she might get cut in the first round.

"What's that, Forbes?" The blowhard studio exec yells into my ear.

"Nothing." A gusty sigh of relief escapes me as the judge taps her ill-fated partner on the shoulder.

Jade stares after the woebegone young man as he leaves. She slips her hand into some sort of pocket, pulls out a little vial, squirts something into her palm, and rubs her hands together in swift, economical gestures. I can see her mouth moving.

What is she doing? Some sort of good luck charm? A hex of

some kind? Maybe it's just hand sanitizer—but the middle of the dance floor seems like a weird time for that. Maybe this has something to do with the 'emotional problems' she hinted at in yesterday's interview. I'm wondering if they have anything to do with Pearl. Having a sister like Pearl would mess any girl up.

Jade rejoins the second milling pack of fifty, waiting nervously on the sidelines for their turn to be sifted. This process will go on until we have the top twenty, ten women and ten men, and then we'll run them in combined pairs through the various styles, letting the public decide who advances, until the final winners are left standing.

Jade finds and speaks to her friend Alex. The two make a nice-looking couple, and I hope they're enjoying the surprise of the suite I reserved for them. I shouldn't be so relieved Alex is gay. It's none of my business who she hooks up with. Though she doesn't really seem the kind for hooking up...

"So what, Forbes?" The exec booms at me, and I leave the distraction of the window and refocus on keeping the show going.

I resist the urge to call my assistant producer and get Jade marked forward to the top twenty. I could justify that move by the ratings she'll generate in the finals with the 'sister of Pearl' angle—but if anyone ever found out I did, it would smirch her reputation.

She'd hate getting any advantage because of Pearl. She'd hate *me*. And I don't want her to hate me.

CHAPTER SIX

Jade

I'M SO TIRED BY THE end of Day One of the show that I realize that I've never really had to work this hard at dance before. Even when I started, as late as everyone keeps harping on, I was the fastest to pick things up in every class. I'd see a move done, register what it was, count and analyze the steps or move, and could almost always reproduce what I saw. I had good, solid instruction in ballet, modern, and jazz styles from Jo-Ann Curtola, the mistress in charge of the Eureka Dance Studio. She's been a mentor for years, and I her star pupil—eventually teaching classes at the studio, as well.

What I've never experienced before is a competitive dance situation with peers. For the show, I'm surrounded by people my age who've been dancing their whole lives, and their passion to succeed burns as bright and hot as mine. It's intense to be in the same room with so much talent, and to see the contestants getting culled right and left. Everywhere, the cameras, on rolling stands, move among us: capturing the smiles, the tears, the sprained ankles, and the drama.

I'm terrified that the cameras are going to catch me cleaning my hands, hiding a tiny bottle of sanitizer in my waistband and stealthily using it.

Five judges move through and around the groups of dancers, cutting people right and left. They aren't the same ones, the famous ones that I performed for, seated behind a table at the tryouts. No, these are seasoned dance instructors, and they're ruthless.

I never spot Forbes even once as the endless day unwinds, and I tell myself that it doesn't matter. He's the show's main producer, so I'm sure he has more important things to do than pay attention to this level of the competition.

Even Alex's golden complexion has gone sallow with stress and fatigue by the end of the day, as we ride the elevator to our suite.

"That was a little slice of hell," Alex flicks imaginary sweat off his forehead dramatically. "I had no idea we'd have to fight so hard just to stay in the running on day one. There are some damn good dancers on this show."

"Yeah. Tomorrow's going to be much the same—they got rid of a hundred people today." I bend over and set my palms on the floor, stretching my aching lower back.

"It's going to be mobbed. We have a giant Jacuzzi tub in our suite. Let's invite Sheila, Keilie, Judd, and that cutie Ernesto up to join us." Being the fun, outgoing guy Alex is, he's making tons of friends. I've been as friendly as I'm able, but can't say I met a single person I'm eager to spend any more time with.

Except Brandon Forbes.

I didn't just have that thought. I squint my eyes shut. "Sure," I say, though I am going to have to have another of those tiny vodka bottles from the minibar to get in the mood to deal with more people.

Alex keys open the door of our suite. "Holy shit," he exclaims. "Check this out."

A huge fancy picnic basket adorns the coffee table in front of the couches. We both advance to look down at a wicker hamper filled with treats: a box of truffles, fresh pears, expensive cheeses and salami, two kinds of crackers, and even a pot of caviar.

"There's a card." Alex plucks it off the plastic holder. "I'm guessing it's from your guy, so you can open it."

"He's not my guy," I say automatically, but my heart is thudding with excitement as I open the tiny envelope. *"Congratulations on making it to the next round! ~Brandon Forbes"* is written in a bold, slanting hand, a mix of block letters and cursive that I want to keep reading over and over.

"We're definitely partying now," Alex picks up a pear, tosses it high, and bites into it. "We have extra tasty food."

"I don't think we should let the others know about this," I say, sliding the card inside my bra, where I can feel it poking me. *He signed it himself.* A happy little glow begins somewhere in my tummy. "I doubt everyone got a congratulations basket."

A picnic basket is the perfect gift. Thoughtful without being romantic, it's ideal for dancers eating like horses who shouldn't drink alcohol before another big day of athletics. It's the perfect supportive gesture, and the card embraces both of us.

Brandon Forbes is a classy guy.

"Maybe you're right. When we have dinner downstairs—let's see if anyone else is staying in a penthouse suite and getting food baskets from the big boss." Alex licks pear juice off his chin. "Oh wait. I'm pretty sure that's just us."

"He might get in trouble if the other contestants found out we were being treated differently." I almost can't bear to say the words. "I don't want you telling anyone."

Alex goes still and silent, staring at me with wide eyes. "Do you think he's protecting us from the judges?"

"No. No. I don't think so," I rub my hands up and down my tights. "I never saw him all day and those judges were like sharks feeding on the weak."

"Because—and I hate to say this, and put a dimmer on your very real talent—but I bet having you in the final twenty would be good for ratings. Once they air that interview about you being Pearl's sister—everyone's going to be curious about you and want to see what you do."

"Oh geez." I'm rubbing my hands together nonstop now. I have to wash. I run into the bathroom, turn on the tap, pump soap into my hands twice, rub my hands together thirteen times, and pass them back and forth under the water thirteen times.

Alex follows me in. "What are you doing?"

"Washing my hands calms me down." I start another round of washing.

"You got OCD or something?"

"Of course not."

"Well, whatever." Alex has other things on his mind. "We need to shut down this preferential treatment. If we move ahead in the competition and anyone else gets wind of it, we could be disqualified." Alex stretches his quads, addressing me in the mirror.

"But who's going to disqualify us if the owner and producer of the show is the one giving us a few perks?" I feel compelled to play devil's advocate. "I mean, Forbes is in charge. This is his show."

"But it would look bad if someone takes issue with it. Someone could sue or something, say the contest was rigged." Alex puts his hands on his hips. "I'm surprised the dude doesn't know better, quite frankly. This is the show's third season." Alex seems to be building up a head of steam. "I want you to find out where his room is and take that picnic basket back. And we'll ask for a regular room. Much as it pains me, it's the right thing to do."

I begin a third round of hand washing. I'm going to need a full thirteen to get through this. "You wouldn't make me go alone."

"Okay, I'll go with you. But you have to do all the talking. Because if you think this is about me, you're even more naïve than I took you for."

"That's not nice," I say. "Really not nice." I stick my tongue out at him.

"Well, I'm having another one of those pears and calling Patty to find out where his room is while you finish your hand washing. And don't wear the skin off while you're at it. Someone might get the idea you have OCD or something."

Brandon

I'm just getting to the end of a workout, on my second round of pushups, when the doorbell chimes with the room service I ordered.

I jump up and pull open the door without checking the peep-hole—and come up short. Jade's standing there, almost hidden by the huge, stupid picnic basket I couldn't resist sending to her room because I was so relieved that she'd made it to the next round.

Her eyes flicker down, and then up, and I realize I'm only wearing those damn tight athletic pants, no shirt.

"Oh, hey. Didn't expect you." I decide to brazen it out rather than running off to find a shirt—after all, I'm here in my room alone, working out, minding my own business. More importantly —does she like what she sees? I'm not as chiseled as a male dancer, but I make up for that with bulk. I lean an arm on the doorjamb and flex my abs, trying for casual. "What're you doing here?" Like I don't know she's returning the damn basket.

"I...I had to bring this back." Jade steps forward and thrusts the basket into my midsection so hard it knocks me off balance. "We can't accept this. Preferential treatment will look bad."

I do not take the basket even though the wicker is stabbing me in the belly. "Throw it in the trash, then." I liked thinking of her eating one of those juicy pears. Disappointment and rejection tighten my stomach.

Jade sets the basket on the ground at my feet. "Alex and I— we talked it over. We can't be treated any different than the other contestants." She looks wildly over her shoulder toward the elevator. The Puerto Rican kid probably came with her, but now I see that the elevator doors have shut and the numbers are changing above the door. "And we need a regular room, too," Jade says breathlessly.

I'm prepared for this. I hold my slouching stance, head cocked, eyes at half-mast. "I think the hotel is booked. Did you have a problem with your room?" I push the basket back across the threshold toward her with a foot. "Too bad you didn't care for the basket. Just thought I'd be supportive of the winners of this round of the competition. If you ask around, you'll discover that everyone who moved ahead got them." Yeah, it cost me a fortune to have all those baskets sent, but I couldn't single her out. I'm not an idiot. Still, no one else got a card signed by me, that's for damn sure.

I don't know why Jade interests me so much—is it just because of Pearl? I'm still not sure.

The color drains out of Jade's face. Her hands come up to cup her cheeks. "Oh geez, I'm so embarrassed. And the room was...just because the hotel is full?"

"What is this about your room? Is there a problem with it?" I frown as if confused. "I'm the producer of the show. You should be talking to Patty." Patty Scandling is the manager in charge of the dancers and their needs. "Her info should have been in your contest packet, but I can get you her extension." I push away from the door and leave it open, hoping she will follow me in.

She doesn't.

Over by the desk, I call out. "Come in a minute, and we'll figure this out together."

Jade picks up the basket and wraps both arms around it like she's gone overboard and it's a flotation device. Her face is bright red now.

"I was mistaken," she murmurs, walking across the carpet as if it's a minefield. "I'm so sorry. This is embarrassing."

I jot down Patty's extension. "You have any problems with the food, medications, your room, etcetera, Patty's the gal to get ahold of."

Jade's standing right in front of me now, wearing her ballet gear from the day. Her French braid is unraveling around the edges. Her cheeks are pink. She has one of those glass faces that shows everything she's feeling.

Damn, she's cute. I smile and reach out to take one of the pears from the basket.

"Since you brought the basket back, though, you might as well share." I take a big, juicy bite.

"Oh, thanks so much. I thought you were feeling sorry for me because of Pearl or something, and I thought... oh God." Jade puts her forehead against the wicker handle of the basket and presses so hard it makes a dent in her skin. "I'll just go now." She whirls and heads for the door.

I take three giant strides and beat her to it, holding up the pear to block her way. "Hey now. Not so fast." I remove the basket from her hands. "I can see how you might have had that impression if your room was inappropriate in some way. It's no big deal, and I'm not offended." I smile big, but not too much teeth—don't want to spook her. "I just finished my workout and was going to hop in the shower. I've got room service on the way. I could sure use some company. It's lonely at the top, you know."

Jade looks taken aback: eyes wide, mouth ajar. I don't want her to muster enough brainpower to come up with excuses, so I walk over to the table and set the basket on it firmly.

"Great. Thanks for staying. I want to hear your impressions of the judging process." I head for the bathroom. "And let the room service guy in if he comes, will ya? He'll just go away if I don't answer the door, and then I'd lose my meal."

She wouldn't run off and leave me without food.

I hope.

I take the fastest shower in the history of fast showers but realize I didn't bring in any clothes, and the hotel robe is hanging in my bedroom. I'm going to have to walk out of the bathroom in a towel. Hopefully she won't faint.

I wonder if she's as inexperienced and shy as she seems.

Couldn't be, with a sister like Pearl. But didn't she stay with the mom and grandparents, while Pearl went to live with Ruby because she was in so much trouble? I dry off and wrap the towel around my waist, opening the door.

"Be right out," I say in Jade's direction as I head for the bedroom. I register that the room service cart is parked by the table. I make it to the bedroom and shut the door.

"Please be there when I get out," I whisper. Because it really is lonely at the top.

Jade

I don't look at Brandon as he walks by only wearing a towel.

Or I try not to. I can't help a tiny peek.

The view isn't much more overwhelming than him, all shiny

with sweat, bulky and ripped, no shirt on, leaning against the doorjamb.

Except that now he's only wearing a towel—which could fall off.

And leave him wearing nothing at all.

I swallow as he tells me that he'll be right out and the bedroom door shuts. It's almost like he cares whether or not I'm there when he comes out.

I can't believe I'm still here.

I should just leave. But maybe Brandon really does want some company, and if I can get past the awful faux pas that brought me here…At least I intercepted the room service cart and brought it inside.

There's a covered carafe of red wine on the cart, and a glass, and whatever he ordered is on a plate under one of those silver dome things. I get his place setting ready for something to do: aligning the heavy silver knife and fork on a silky white napkin on the table. I put the carafe and the glass above the silverware and place the covered plate on the table. I sit down in a chair beside his.

His dinner smells delicious. Alex and I never took showers or ate after we decided to return the picnic basket, and my stomach growls loudly.

Brandon walks out of the bedroom, still buttoning his shirt, which gives me a second of regret as his amazing abs are hidden. The grin that breaks over his face looks genuine. "You're still here. Thanks for keeping me company."

"I just want to—you know. Apologize again. For being such an imbecile."

"Imbecile. Now that's a word you don't hear every day. I like it." He sits down in front of the food and immediately frowns. "But I didn't know you were coming, and I only ordered for one."

"Oh, no. I'm not hungry." But the smell wafting up from

under the silver dome makes my stomach growl again. He stares pointedly at my middle and I laugh. "Okay, I'm a little hungry. Alex and I were going to drop off the picnic basket and go down to the dining hall next."

"We can make this work. Bust out what's in the basket and we'll divide this up."

I pull the basket over as he lifts the lid off the plate, uncovering a huge rib eye steak, fragrant and juicy, with a baked potato and a generous pile of broccoli on the side.

I actually moan at the sight. "Oh, dang, that looks so good."

"And it'll taste good too. Look through that basket and find some other stuff we can round off the plates with." He's already sawing the steak in half.

I hunt through the basket. "Got salami and cheese and crackers. We can have the fruit and chocolate for dessert."

"That'll work." Brandon halves everything that was on his plate and sorts a portion onto the bread plate that came with the meal. He gets up and fetches a water glass from the sink and fills it with wine. I busy myself cutting off pieces of cheese and salami and dividing them onto the two plates along with the fancy crackers.

His stomach emits a loud rumble, and mine does too. We laugh, and it's the first moment I don't feel awkward and terrified. He hands me the nice wine glass, filled with ruby red liquid, and picks up the water glass. "To surviving day one."

"Cheers."

We clink glasses and sip. The wine's delicious: light and fruity, with just a little tang to keep things interesting. He pushes the bigger plate of food over to me.

I push it back. "Oh no. This is your dinner I'm crashing. Besides, I shouldn't have that many calories."

"I'm the boss. This is yours." He pushes it back.

"Oh, you're going to play that card already?" I find myself smiling. "Trying to ruin my chances by weighing me down?"

"Just want to see you eat." The tops of his ears go red. "If your waist gets any smaller it's going to be the size of my arm, not my thigh."

He's been comparing my body to his. That shouldn't be as sexy as it is.

I don't like him that way. *He's Pearl's ex.* I really have to focus to keep that unpleasant fact in mind.

There is only one set of silverware, but he cuts up my steak so I don't need anything. I can't bring myself to touch the food with my fingers because of germs, so I find a toothpick on the cart. I poke a cube of steak and pop it into my mouth, chewing.

"Ooh," I moan, shutting my eyes. "This is the best steak ever."

Brandon is efficiently mowing through his steak, too. I try not to keep moaning...but it's hard to stay quiet as I pick up each fragrant, juicy chunk of meat and pop it into my mouth. I'm pretty sure I've never tasted anything so delicious. Mere minutes later, we've finished the beef, potato, and broccoli. Brandon sits back and takes a sip of wine.

"That hit the spot. Would have been too much food for one person, anyway."

"I still have a little room for cheese and crackers." I lean back and burp a little behind my fist. "Excuse me."

"Remember, you started this." Brandon lets rip with a really big burp, and we both laugh. I drink my wine, and we move on to the cheese, crackers, and salami.

"So tell me more about yourself," Brandon says. "Pearl never talked much about you and your mom."

"You know, I'd rather you started first." I sit back with the wine glass, swirling it like I've seen connoisseurs do. "She never told me about you at all."

"Ouch." He winces comically. That he can clown around

about Pearl makes me hope he's over the hurt she dealt him. "Okay. I rescued Pearl from a mugger in Boston. And when I got her home, I was shocked by how beautiful she was. I wanted to impress her, so I dragged her off to meet my mother, Melissa, who owns a well-known modeling agency. The rest is history."

"So it was you that gave her the big break into modeling?" The wine is making me feel pleasantly warm and loose in the knees. "I wondered how that happened. I was so miserable back then, trying to get used to California and in my first year of high school... it just seemed so unfair that my sister was suddenly traveling the world, her face everywhere."

"Modeling's not as glamorous as it seems." Brandon turns toward me. He leans over and takes hold of my ankle. I gasp as he lifts my foot onto his thigh and removes my ballet slipper.

"Just as I suspected. Look at these blisters!" He inspects my toes, reddened and bruised from the exertions of the day. His thumb digs into the sole of my foot, his fingers grasping the top of it firmly so I can't pull it away. "People think dancing is so glamorous. But they don't see all the ways that it's one of the most physically challenging things any human can do." Both of his thumbs are massaging the sole of my foot now.

I tip my head back against the back of the chair and groan with pleasure. I clap a hand over my mouth. "Sorry. It just feels so good."

"That's okay. Shut your eyes. Relax. You worked hard today."

My eyes fall shut as I lean back against the chair. I'm too full and too tired to resist being made to feel this good. I settle deeper, my spine bending in a deep curve as he picks up my other foot. He removes my slipper, and sets both of my feet on his thighs.

Brandon rubs deep into tension stored in the arches of my feet that I didn't even know was there. I sigh with ecstasy and feel myself melting. Delicious feeling sends shivers of pleasure up my legs. Oh, this feels so good...I'm drifting away, actually falling asleep.

I suddenly remember how sweaty my feet must be.

I never had a shower. They must smell.

They're loaded with germs.

My eyes fly open. I've slid halfway down the chair. My feet are deep in his lap, almost touching his crotch as his big hands massage them. Brandon's green-gold eyes are intense on my face.

I yank my feet out of his hands, blood heating my cheeks. "I'm so sorry! I never had a shower. My feet must be so gross."

Brandon's gaze tells me he wasn't thinking about foot odor and germs. "Doesn't bother me." He picks up the big dinner napkin and drops it in his lap. "Now, where were we? Give me that foot."

"Oh, no! You've done too much already. Thanks for the dinner. And the basket, too." I jump up and grab the empty basket, hugging it to my chest, as I wriggle my feet into my slippers. "I really need to get back to my room and get cleaned up."

Brandon stands up too, still holding the napkin in front of his lap. "Thanks for joining me. It was much nicer having company than eating alone." He follows me to the door. "See you tomorrow, Jade."

"Thanks again, Brandon." I hope he likes the way his name sounds when I say it as much as I like how he says mine. "I hope I'll still be around tomorrow."

"I have faith in you. Sleep well." He shuts the door behind me gently and firmly.

CHAPTER SEVEN

Brandon

MELISSA CALLS ON THE CORDLESS as I'm standing at the window the next day, watching the kaleidoscope of dancers below as the contest moves through the second day of competition. "Hello, Mother."

"I wish you would just call me Melissa." She sounds distracted, like it's a knee-jerk response and her heart isn't really in it. "How's the show going?"

"We're well underway. Looks like the judges will be getting rid of another fifty or so today, so we're on schedule."

"Any interesting talent?"

"There's always interesting talent. I like to wait longer to see who's shaping up."

"I know you do. But do you see any modeling talent in this group?"

"No six foot standouts, no, if that's what you're looking for."

Melissa sighs. "You know what I'm looking for. That one perfect Pearl in the sea."

"Ha. Ha." I pronounce each word distinctly. "This is a dance show, Mother."

"I know. And just because they get cut from the competition doesn't mean there might not be some print possibilities there."

"You want to come out and roll an eye over the herd? Tell you the truth, I haven't had time to be your talent scout with this show." I pick up a folder of applications and headshots. "You could always send your assistant down."

"I think I might do that." She sighs.

"What's the matter, Mother?"

"I had some tests." Her voice is small. "I have a lump in my breast."

I set down the folder, frowning. "What? What do they think it is?"

"Not sure yet. They found this lump during my annual mammogram; and now I'm having extra tests."

"What kind of tests?" My heart rate spikes. Dad died when I was ten. Things may not be all that great between Mom and me, but she's my only family.

"A needle biopsy. Next week."

I ask some more questions: what doctor, when, when will she know the results, etcetera—the questions you're supposed to ask at a time like this. I feel numb, like my mouth is moving and words are coming out, but the conversation is happening to someone else.

"Don't worry." Her voice is soft now. "I'm sure it's going to be fine. You're the best thing in my life, you know." She hangs up with a soft click.

I stare at the phone in my hand.

The best thing in her life? I thought that was her business: the careers and faces she's put on billboards.

Melissa must really be rattled by this.

I walk over to the window and gaze down at the crowd,

searching through it without knowing what I'm looking for—until I find it.

Jade's wearing black ballet gear today: a long sleeve, scoop neck leotard paired with black tights and a filmy black wrap skirt. Her hair is in a tightly coiled bun. She's doing some sort of slide and shimmy jazz routine with a group of about twenty girls.

I got her to eat last night.

And burp.

And moan.

I liked the little noises she made over her steak so much that I got her to do more of them by rubbing her feet. I loved watching her in the chair, making those sexy sounds. She relaxed so much that she almost fell asleep.

Jade would understand how scary it is to have this happening to my only parent. Her dad died when she was just a little older than I'd been when mine passed. Watching her dance makes me feel better about my mom somehow.

The phone rings again. I watch Jade for a few seconds more and then go answer it.

"Forbes."

"Brandon?" The woman's voice on the line is very familiar, and lifts the hairs on my arms with its husky tone. I should have forgotten how her voice sounds by now.

"Who is this?" I pretend I don't know, maintaining the impatient business tone I answered with.

"This is Pearl. Pearl Michaels."

Pearl Michaels. The woman I rescued, discovered, made famous, and fell in love with. International supermodel.

Jade's sister.

"Oh, hey, Pearl." I switch to casual. "I never wished you congratulations on your wedding."

She laughs deprecatingly. "We eloped. It was very quiet. But thanks."

"So what can I do for you today?" I switch back to business impatient. This woman crushed me so badly I'm still not sure I'm over it—the kind of maiming that leaves you missing a limb and suffering ghost pain long after.

"Is—my sister there?"

I'm blank for a moment. Of course. She's calling for Jade. "How'd you get this number?"

"I have a few connections." Pearl switches to businesslike as well. "I'm calling to see if my sister Jade is competing on your dance show."

"As a matter of fact, she is. Doing rather well, too." I walk over to the window and look down. Her partner has her overhead in a lift, but something goes wrong. I gasp as they wipe out, knocking over several other dancers as they hit the ground in a spectacular wipeout.

"What's wrong?" Pearl's voice goes high with alarm.

"Just a little slip-up on the dance floor. I'm monitoring from the office." I watch to see if Jade gets up from the tangle of arms and legs she landed in. Injuries are terrifying in this competition. They've sidelined many a legitimate contender. Jade scrambles to her feet, shaking out one leg. Her partner stands more slowly, and he's favoring an ankle. She hugs him and kneels to look at it. "Carnage on the battlefield. Yes, she's a contestant."

"I called because she ran off for the auditions. She left a note and a phone message, but Mom is worried sick."

"Well, Jade's fine." At least she seems to be, at the moment, though her partner, a sturdy young black man, is not. With Jade on one side and one of the judges on the other, he's being assisted off the competition floor.

She's going to feel responsible. I should check up on them.

"You won't...hurt her chances because of me?" Pearl's sexy voice is low and hesitant.

"What?" For the first time I really focus on the conversation.

62

I walk back to my desk and sit down. "You think I would bias the judges against Jade because of *you*? Wow. That shows how little you ever knew me."

A long moment passes. Pearl sighs out a breath. "I'm sorry. Again. For even thinking that. I just worry about Jade, and she'll never let me do anything to help. She's had it rough. She has issues. Please, just cut her some slack."

"She doesn't need any slack from me or anyone. Jade is an extraordinary dancer. I don't think you know how talented she is." I feel a bubble of pride tighten my chest—pride in the strength, resilience and talent of the youngest Michaels girl.

"That's good to hear. Because of course she never wanted me to come to any of her performances." Pearl's voice is tight with hurt. "But I'm glad I called. Now I know that she's safe."

These sisters are in need of some sort of reckoning, but I'm no family therapist. That reminds me—I want to know about those 'issues' Jade has that keep getting hinted at. "What's wrong with Jade? What issues does she have?"

"If you can't tell what they are, then they aren't a problem," Pearl says smoothly.

I smile. Pearl might be hurt by her sister, but she called out of concern, embarrassed herself with me, and now she's refusing to throw her little sister under the bus. I like that— she's loyal.

"All right. I hope Jade makes it through to the top twenty. If she does, I'll send tickets for all of you to come watch the competition at the studio."

"Oh, would you?" The excitement in Pearl's voice reminds me of holding her in my arms. She was like an ivory candle, throwing off heat and light. Unforgettable. "That would mean so much to us. Please, do keep me posted—and ask Jade to call me." Pearl rattles off her personal number. I make a note of it automatically.

I don't want to have Pearl's personal number. I fold the paper in half so as not to look at it. "Goodbye, Pearl."

I hang up, feeling gutted.

It was all good until that last bit, when I remembered what it felt like to run with Pearl through the streets of Venice, to see her go from the dark and damaged girl I rescued on the bank of the Charles River to the international beauty she was meant to be.

Until I remembered what it was like to hold Pearl in my arms and kiss her. We never did more than that, but with Pearl, that was enough.

I'm not over Pearl, after all. Damn it.

I walk back to the window and look down into the mass of dancers. *Jade's gone.*

Screw both of the Michaels sisters. I've got work to do.

Jade

"That's a wrap!" The energetic director, Alan Bowes, bellows into a megaphone. I'm so exhausted that I slide down into splits, and lie facedown on the floor to really open up my hip sockets.

"That's not a position the family jewels appreciate." Alex's got an arm hooked around the neck of his hunky friend Ernesto, a slender, ripped dancer whose main ethnicity might be Native American, guessing by his straight black hair, tawny skin, and bladelike cheekbones. He and Alex seem headed in a romantic direction.

"We made it through another day," I say.

"Yeah. Thank God. Rough one today." Alex shakes his head.

"Did you see my partner Henry go down? I felt so bad. Sprained his ankle lifting my fat butt, and he's out of the competition." I slide my legs over into scissors splits.

"You know your butt isn't fat, and it could be any one of us next. Gonna come up to the room?" Alex asks.

"I'll stay down here and do some stretches. When Henry wiped out, I banged my knee and hip pretty good." I roll up my ankle-length tights to show them the knee, already purpling up. Icing it helped. I was lucky though—there wasn't any deeper tissue damage.

Not like poor Henry. If I was lighter, if I didn't jump so hard into the lift...

The guys move off with a salute and a wave. I bend my head forward to touch my damaged knee, breathing into the stretch, willing my ligaments to relax even as I feel a twinge from my bruised hip. I crave solitude to unwind, and the cavernous floor of the studio is emptying out rapidly. I'm just not used to sharing my life with so many people.

Finally, it's only me in the great open space, and I sigh with relief.

I roll onto my back and flip my legs up over my head to stretch my back. I close my eyes. Breathe. Nothing going on but the rush of blood in my ears and the sound of my heartbeat.

And then the sound of shoes on the echoing floor. Not a dancer, with that definite stride, staccato and hard. I hope he's not approaching me—but no such luck.

"Jade."

It's Brandon. My eyes pop open and I flip over onto my knees, then wince. "Ow." I stand up gracelessly, trying not to favor my knee.

He's backlit and his face looks closed and remote, with none of the warmth of last night. He's holding something out to me—a slip of paper. I take it automatically. "Your sister called. Here's her number. She wants you to call back." His voice is icy.

"How's Ruby?" I should have thought of calling my big sister before, but I wanted to make it to the Top Twenty before I talked to anyone from the family.

"It was Pearl who called." Brandon turns with a fluidity that tells me he could have been a dancer too. He walks away, those hard business shoes echoing on the floor.

Pearl called for me? The thought won't compute. I open my hand and look at the slip of paper, one edge ragged where he tore it off of something larger. *PEARL* is written in bold, slanting block letters, and a string of numbers.

I gaze at his ramrod straight retreating back. An overhead light gilds his short blond hair as he leaves the studio area, disappearing down the hall. Fifteen words, that's all he spoke to me, not one more than he needed to use to convey a message—and now I know he's not over her.

Really not over her. *At all.*

I blink and blink, looking down at the slip of paper in my hand. "It doesn't matter. It's fine. As long as he doesn't take it out on me on the show, it's fine," I tell myself aloud. "It's not like I liked him or anything."

The stab of pain in my chest tells me different. It's hard to believe that just yesterday Brandon shared his dinner with me and rubbed my feet.

I take the elevator to our room. I can tell by the discarded towels and piled dancewear that the boys showered and went down to dinner—and probably more socializing. The thought makes my stomach ache.

I take a shower and find an Ace bandage in my gear bag. Probably too late for any ice to make a difference.

I pop a few ibuprofen, braid my hair... and find I'm too tired and heartsick to go downstairs and deal with more people and eat. *No, not heartsick.* Tired. Numb. Sleep is what I need.

I finish the cheese and the last pear in the picnic basket, and go to bed.

CHAPTER EIGHT

Brandon

I TAKE MY PLACE NEXT TO the director in our spot below the film stage and lean over. "How's it going?"

Alan Bowes should be a cliché, but he's unabashedly himself —gleaming head, leather, chrome jewelry and all. A former dancer, he knows what he's looking for to continue to keep tension high on the show. The last few days have been a bloodbath of drama.

"Excellent." Alan gives me a thumbs up. "Ready to roll the top twenty couples announcement."

I sit back in my canvas Producer chair, making busy with the clipboard of to-dos and signature reviews that my assistant hands me.

It's been two days since I spoke to Jade and gave her Pearl's number. The next couple of days, I rolled down the blind in the upstairs office and made a concerted effort to pay attention to my job: making sure every stage of the competition was covered and storyboarded, sponsors were lined up and happy, the sound stage guy who was out sick was covered.

Our numbers are good, building as we head toward the big Top Twenty show.

And I've made no effort to find out how Jade is doing—nor even to see who's going to be in the Top Twenty.

Because it really doesn't matter. Whoever it is, the show will go on—and it's the show that's important.

Of course, Alan is spinning out the agony with a group performance. Then, dividing the group for another performance. These poor kids have been practicing their hearts out, getting cut and not knowing it, for the last forty-eight hours.

A professional troupe of former *Dance, Dance, Dance* competitors comes on and blows minds with a breakdance, foxtrot, and ballet segment.

Finally, it's time for the Top Twenty announcement.

They pull the dancers out of groups of ten, leaving five from each group on stage after bowing the rest off, and at last the process is over. Jade and her buddy Alex are hugging each other and jumping up and down, crying openly, as a barrel of confetti dumps on the contestants' heads and strobe lights scythe around the stage.

I let out a long, slow breath that I didn't even know I was holding.

"Got any favorites?" I lean over to ask Alan as the top twenty competitors fold each other in the kind of emotional group hug only people between the ages of eighteen and twenty-two are prone to. I'm only twenty-seven but I feel like a jaded old man already.

Alan grins. "I might. But I'm not going to jinx their chances by saying any names out loud. It's up to the public now, and it's not just how good they dance—it's how well they engage the audience."

And that might be hard for Jade, with those "issues" she has.

She's certainly an awkward little thing when she's not dancing. I squelch a stab of worry.

I stand up abruptly. "Got some stuff to take care of. Got to line up the individual spotlights."

We do a short feature segment on each of the top twenty. It's time to exploit that connection between Pearl and Jade for the cameras. Maybe I should call Pearl, after all. Get a sound bite.

My stomach tightens. I don't want to speak to Pearl for any reason. But I can have an assistant do it. Do the whole thing, in fact. I head back to the office area above the big open dance floor where the dancers practice, and make a quick call to my mom.

Melissa has that artificially bright note in her voice that tells me she's putting a good face on something when I call her. "The biopsy went well. They think they got a good sample."

"That's great, Mother. When will you know?"

"Not until next week."

We sit with that a moment. "So. I didn't send my assistant, and you have your top twenty. I just got done watching—great show. And I saw Jade Michaels made it through." Her voice is carefully neutral.

"So she did."

"And you didn't have anything to do with that?"

"Of course not, Mother." I stride back and forth in front of the darkened viewing window, pushing a hand through my hair. "I don't get in the way of the judges."

"Well. There's already a lot of interest in Jade. The camera loves her." I hear a rustling. "Found a piece speculating on her chances in this morning's Arts and Culture section of the New York Times."

"People will speculate." I peer out the window. Someone's moving around in the big open space below.

"I think she has potential now that I've watched her on the show. I want you to sign her with The Melissa Agency."

"No," I say automatically. Forcefully.

"What?"

"No. She's too short." It's all I can think of. I don't want Melissa getting her hooks into Jade—no idea why. It certainly was a good thing for Pearl. I squint. No lights are on in the room below, but I can see someone's down there. Dancing, from the graceful, rhythmic movements, just a blot of dark against slightly less dark.

"We're branching out. Commercials. Catalogs. Print. I'm even thinking about acting. She'll be good for something. Like I said, the camera loves her."

"You can handle that yourself, then, Mother. Let me know when you hear the results." I hang up the phone, both irritated and concerned. The office's window is covered with one-way reflective tinting, but still I lower the blind and flick off the light. The kids aren't supposed to use the studio after hours, and dancing in the dark is downright dangerous.

Jade

I can't contain the ecstatic joy of making it to the next level. All I wanted to do, after all the crazy screaming, crying, jumping, and hysteria at the end of the show, was to get to the big empty space of the studio and express all the feelings surging through my body.

I'm at the studio, hand on the door, when I realize that I got all the way through the show, the gut-wrenching anxiety, and even all the touching—without using my hand sanitizer once.

It must mean something. Maybe I'm getting better. "In vivo exposure" is one of the treatment methods for OCD—they overwhelm you with stuff and then don't let you wash. Perhaps that's what's happening to me.

The door of the studio is open. That must mean something too. It's usually locked after hours. There's a light on in the office upstairs, but I can't see in even with it dark below. Someone probably forgot and left a light on up there.

The vast open space calls to me and I leap into it, a grin of joy stretching my face wide with unfiltered happiness.

I did it. I made it to the top twenty!

I leap across the vast space, finding some depth of leftover energy, and as I soar through the darkness, the most exquisite bliss overtakes me. I did a hard thing on my own, and beat the odds.

I pause for a moment, panting, and pull the bobby pins out of my heavy bun, sliding them onto the scooped neck of my leotard. I scrub my fingers across my aching scalp—ah, the relief—and then I spin.

I once did twenty-eight continuous spins, pumping a leg in and out to keep going. Today I make it to twenty-six, arms extended, hair flying—and it feels so good that I laugh at the end as I sink down into splits, spread my arms, and lay my cheek on the floor.

Screw the germs.

I just lie there, head to the side, eyes closed... and the last of the tension ebbs away, flowing out of my hip sockets, down my legs, and out of my toes.

"You're not supposed to be here after hours." Brandon Forbes's voice is right above me. His voice is just as frosty as the last time he spoke fifteen whole words to me. I squeak in alarm, roll to the side, and stand up.

"How did you sneak up on me like that?" I sound snappy and defensive, even to my own ears.

"I came to tell whoever was down here that the studio is closed. Which you know, I'm sure."

"I'm sorry. I just needed—to dance a little bit." I hurry toward the exit. Misery cramps my belly. One call from Pearl was all it took to make him hate me.

"Did you call your sister?" He must be reading my mind. He's walking after me, and must be wearing moccasins or something because I can't hear those ugly shoes on the floor.

"No, I did not." I don't tell him that I called Mom and Ruby instead, and we had a good talk. I have no desire whatsoever to talk to Pearl, and besides, my family is none of his damn business.

I push open the door just as Brandon puts a hand on my arm. The hallway light, a low-wattage bulb that's always on, falls over us and feels as bright as a strobe after the soothing dark. Whatever he was going to say seems to die on his lips as he looks at me. His eyes are hidden from the harsh light in caves of darkness, and I can't see what's in them.

"Your hair is down. I wondered what you'd look like with your hair down." One of his hands is still on my arm. The other skims the length of my hair, touches my waist light as a moth. "I like it."

I should be upset that he's touching me. That he thought about my hair—down or up, it's none of his business. But my heart is hammering too hard to think about anything but how close he is, how much I want to see what the expression is in his shadowed eyes. I take a step closer and let go of the door, which swings shut silently and surrounds us in darkness again. Our bodies brush. The heat between us vibrates like electricity, raising the fine hairs of my arms, prickling my nipples into tightness. My face turns up to his, seemingly of its own volition.

"Jade," he breathes into my mouth, and his arms encircle me, light and gentle. His mouth descends to mine.

Oh, this. This. *Oh, this.*

All is darkness, and whirling, and the dimmest pulse of red light. Beating heart, shivering, and sensation drawing me deeper.

Someone gasps—I'm not sure who—but in the muffled sound is surprise, recognition, and surging need.

Hunger.

I bring my arms up to clutch his shoulders, drawing him closer. He tightens his arms, lifting me that six or seven inches in height difference and crushing me close so he can fully taste my mouth.

I give back as good as I'm getting, wrapping my legs around his waist, inching higher so I can kiss him deeper, my arms wrapped around his head, neck, and shoulders. He staggers a few steps to the wall and braces me against it, and I feel like I'm bursting into flames.

"Jade...Jade," he says, and I love the way my name sounds on his lips, how the only thing better than this moment would be to never have to leave it.

I release his mouth so I can tip my head back and feel him kiss my neck, delightful shivery ripples of sensation zinging up and down my spine as he nuzzles deep into the hollow behind my ear with his rough stubble.

"Mmm, you taste so good," he murmurs, lips finding the pulse at the apex of my collarbones. His hands wrap around my bottom, a sensual tension in his grip as he holds me against the wall, and I have to kiss him again.

This time our tongues dance together in an instinctive rhythm—but I'm clumsy, and too eager, and our teeth click together painfully.

He laughs, a deep chuckle. "Slow down," he whispers. "We have all night."

The words wash over me like a draft of cold water.

We don't have all night.

I've never been with a guy before, and it's an ugly embarrassing secret that I don't want him to know—and he had to have slept with Pearl.

How could my clumsy virginity ever compare with going to bed with my beautiful, sexy sister? I'm a freak. I've never met anyone I've liked enough to get past the germs to touch, let alone kiss. Forget having sex. I don't even know how to kiss. My inexperienced groping is all wrong—look how I'm falling all over him!

Shame and embarrassment swamp me, and suddenly my mouth feels alive with germs—terrifying germs. I have to get away. I have to get clean.

I slide my legs down to touch the floor and wrench out of his arms. "I'm sorry. This was a mistake." I use my shoulder to push him away as I dart for the door.

"Jade—let's talk about this!" He reaches for me—but I'm fleeing. I crash through the door and run down the hall, a hand over my mouth as tears fill my eyes.

I'm such a freak. And he's been with my sister. It could never work.

Brandon

Jade is running away from me down the hall, hair streaming behind her like a cape.

I'm such a jerk—I moved way too fast. But she'd seemed so into it...My body is still amped and tingling from touching her. The message that I've been dumped is having a hard time getting to my dick.

I seem to remember Pearl running away from me in Italy, too, the last time I tried to get something going with her.

How the hell did Jade and I end up kissing, anyway?

I shake my head. Probably better she ran off. What a mess.

I use the master key to lock up the studio and take the fifteen flights of stairs to my room on foot, needing to work off angst from the encounter.

Needing to make sense of it somehow.

Pearl's phone call threw me into a funk in the last few days, mulling over my loneliness and even my business partnership and relationship with Mom. More and more, I think I need to totally go out on my own. This show is mine, but I want to run the acting and dance arm of The Melissa Agency, not keep feeding Mom the talent I discover. Like Pearl.

And Jade.

Jade made me dizzy watching her spin as she danced in the dark, just the faintest glow from the exits illuminating her body as she snapped crisply around and around and around, hair whipping. I recognized it was her when she laughed and melted to the floor, letting go of the craziness of the day.

I made my voice hard when I approached her, though, because I still don't know what the hell is going on between us and I'm not sure if my attraction to her is really about Pearl.

Then the light fell over her small figure at the door, lighting that thick dark hair with its red glints... I had to touch it. And the way she turned to me, her face so soft... That was all Jade, herself. Sweet. Inexperienced. Shy.

I never expected the kiss to be such a detonation. Our chemistry just blew up and exploded in both of our faces.

I just want the whole thing to go away somehow.

And yet I don't. I can't stop thinking about her, especially now that I've had a taste of her. She feels so good in my arms—strong and light. Damn, the girl is fine.

Maybe it's just as well she ran away. The last thing I need is another involvement with a Michaels girl.

I reach my floor at last, remembering that I told Pearl I would get her and the family studio tickets if Jade made it to the top twenty. Inside my suite, I head for the clipboard and make a note of it for my assistant.

I might have given Jade Pearl's number, but that didn't keep it from being seared on my brain when I wrote it down.

I head for the shower, and take a cold one.

CHAPTER NINE

Jade

Last night I grabbed a bite to eat at the cafeteria-style dining area of the restaurant that the studio has set up for us, and, in spite of my angst about kissing Brandon, fell asleep like falling down a well.

It's a good thing, too, because the real competition begins today.

We girls drew names and dance styles from a hat this morning. My first partner, dancing the foxtrot, is a guy named Hal from Detroit.

Hal is huge, and looks like a weightlifter in a tee with ripped-off sleeves, but he's surprisingly agile and light on his feet. Turns out he can foxtrot like a champ, which is a good thing since ballroom is my weakest style. Cha-cha and tango I've at least done lessons for, and hip-hop, ballet, and contemporary are all strengths. It sucks to be starting the competition with my weakest performance, but hopefully Hal, nicknamed Twinkletoes halfway through the morning, can move me ahead this round.

We only have one day to learn the dance, then the competition begins filming at six p.m. and runs for two hours.

Halfway through, as Hal and I are back-stepping briskly with our coach, a camera crew arrives. The show's emcee, a style maven named Kate Henley, waves us over. She shoves a mic in our faces. "Hello, beautiful young people. Tell us about yourselves."

I glance at Hal and he winks, turning on some charm I didn't know he had. "I'm Hal. From Detroit. I started dancing at a cotillion when I was thirteen and I haven't looked back since."

"Any specialties?"

"I like ballroom." He's still holding my hand, and spins me under his arm with easy authority, making Kate laugh.

"Well, Hal, you make a nice couple with Jade, here. Jade, we already know fame runs in your family. Tell us what it's like having an international supermodel for a sister?"

"Oh, it's so great," I gush. I anticipated this painful subject would be revisited after Brandon's early interview. "Pearl is so supportive of my dreams. And she's got the pro makeup tips!" I bat my eyes. I remembered to put on a pair of false eyelashes this morning, practically in the dark, because Pearl told me that cameras wash out color and detail—"if you only have time to put on two things, they should be eyelashes and lipstick," she told me once. Not that I listened back then, but today I have on both. I smile big and cock a hip in an exaggerated modeling pose.

"Well, looks and charm certainly run in your family—let's hope dance talent does too!" Kate chirps, and moves on to the next set of victims.

"Your sister is Pearl? *The* Pearl?" Hal's eyes bug out comically. "She's hot. I mean, you're cute and all, but..."

"Yeah, yeah. Try not to flatter me too much." That kind of bumbling comment doesn't even ruffle me; it's happened so often. I sock him in the rock-hard shoulder and take his big sweaty hand in mine, resisting the urge to reach for my hand sanitizer. "Let's get this thing nailed."

Our instructor fires up the music and we get back to practicing. Eventually Wardrobe sends a minion to fetch us.

"I wish we could get our voting call-in numbers printed across our outfits," I tell Hal, holding up the skimpy sequined gown the stylist recommends for me to wear this round. "I don't like this. Reminds me of something from the Ice Capades."

Hal laughs. "Don't care what you pick as long as I don't have to wear tights."

"I totally understand." I hold up a pale pink gown. It has sheer sleeves dotted with rhinestones and a full, calf-length tulle skirt. I can tie my trademark waist ribbon in just the right place. "How do you feel about pink?"

"I rock pink," Hal says with a leer. "Whatever they give me to match you, my manliness can handle it."

I roll my eyes. "Pink it is, then."

I try the dress on, and it fits. I've set myself up with a "trademark" look so that viewers easily recognize me. My partners will just have to go along with it—guys' outfits are so much less complicated.

We practice all the way up until the backstage bell rings, and, while I don't feel super confident, I'm pretty sure Twinkletoes can tuck me under his arm and carry me through the whole thing if necessary.

At the callback, we receive our numbered competition order assignments. Keeping it mixed up is part of the show's dynamic, so we're third in line to perform after a hip-hop and a waltz number, an okay spot.

I explain my "look" to hair and makeup, and I'm pleased with how they do my hair up in a French-braided crown around my head that's studded with rhinestone pins. Several more on flexible, raised wires float above my head, so it seems like there are jewels sparkling above it. Continuing my ballet-influenced ingénue style, makeup goes heavy with false lashes and smoky plum to make my green eyes stand out. Nothing else goes on my face but a few rhinestones on my cheeks and pale pink lip gloss.

The makeup artist paints on the gloss, and I press my lips together. It tastes like strawberry. I picture kissing Brandon, reaching up to hook an arm around his neck, and the way the sweet flavor would be shared... *Where did that thought come from?* I shake my head to get rid of it, and send one of my brilliants flying.

"That's one thing about this hairstyle," the makeup artist says, fetching the bobby pin with its sparkling decoration. "No sudden head movements. Think Queen Victoria."

I laugh as she slides the pin back in. "That will be fine with the foxtrot. Supposed to keep the upper body quiet, anyway."

I hop down off the chair just as Hal comes to the door, resplendent in a black tux sporting a pink bow tie that's the exact shade of my dress.

He whistles long and low. "I take it back. Pearl's got nothing on you, babe."

"Why, thank you." I curtsy, spreading the light, voluminous skirt, and take his arm. We join the other contestants backstage, milling in a nervous herd. I clutch Hal closer. "I'm so freaked out."

"You can grab on me all you like," Hal says, and moves me in front of him so he can cross his big arms over me, both comforting and claiming. The other contestants give us sideways glances.

I like Hal, but not that way. Unfortunately, a certain off-limits show producer has already nailed a stake into my heart. But if it makes us dance better, I'm okay with a little flirting.

I lean back into Hal's solid bulk and try to calm my thundering heart, as couple number one goes out onto the stage.

Brandon

Watching from a high-up glassed-in production booth, television monitors all around, I'm aware of a nice adrenaline buzz. The studio audience is in and seated, primed for excitement and responsiveness with a warm-up dance routine by last year's winners and a funny intro by Kate the emcee—and now, the first couples are up.

The waltz couple performs in the acceptable range; the hip-hop duo is downright dynamic. Jade and her partner appear next, doing the foxtrot.

Jade's in a dress that makes her look like one of those jewelry box dancers that spins when you open the lid, wearing pink so pale it's almost white, sparkles scattered all over it.

The guy she's with is the size of a barn door, but as the music gets going, he's definitely got some moves, handling her with panache... but I don't like the way he keeps that big ham-hand on her waist a little too long.

"Zoom in on camera three," I bark at my assistant. "I want some costume detail."

Her dress has rhinestones scattered all over the clear net arms and up the torso, and Hal Surrey, her partner, keeps his hands technically in the right place for foxtrot—but there's definitely a little something extra going on between them. I check the other monitors. They're looking good—a spin, turn, slide, glide, quick-step and more.

Of the two, Hal is stronger at this step, but Jade is trying hard, throwing herself into it. Her smile up at her partner is so bright it could be a toothpaste commercial.

I feel a nasty little curl of something. Could it be jealousy? Nah. Just indigestion.

They end their session with a terrific move: Jade is lifted overhead and spun by Hal. She looks like a little pink Tinker Bell, held aloft by a big blocky Peter Pan in a tux.

Their finale is met with strong applause. I let out a breath as they go backstage.

"Got a lot more to go," Kerry, my assistant, says. "Take a load off, Boss. You're stressing too much. Everything's going great."

I certainly hope so. These next days are going to be a marathon of dancing for the contestants. We film the whole show in a blitz to keep studio and filming costs down, using the studio audience and random sampling for voting, then parcel out the shows weekly.

We have at least five standout stars from the first round by the end, and sad to say, Jade isn't one of them. Hopefully she's stronger in some other dances, but with fast-stepping Side o'Beef as her partner, she'll probably be able to move to the next round.

We open the phone lines for voting as Alan yells, "that's a wrap!" I check the seats below, looking for Pearl and the rest of Jade's relatives. I had the tickets delivered to their different addresses using an expensive messenger service.

No one is seated in the row reserved for the Michaels family. Twenty-four hours probably was not enough time to get here to Los Angeles from wherever they are on the East Coast.

I check that everything's on track with the editing, and head for the hotel gym to work off the stress of the last few hours.

Jade

In the voting appeal section at the end of the show, I get to see a clip of Hal and my best move, the lift, where he spun me. I have my arms out and toes pointed, like Baby in *Dirty Dancing*. It's a great note to leave in the viewers' minds as we both smile, appealing for viewers to call in and vote for our numbers—and I flash my digits in American Sign Language.

"What was that?" Hal asks as the pulsing eye of the camera moves on to the next couple.

"ASL. Couldn't hurt to help me stand out a little."

"Can you teach me?"

"Sure."

"Now? I kind of need to unwind. Why don't we go to the Jacuzzi, and you can teach me my numbers there?" He wiggles his brows, making it sound naughty.

"Not tonight, Hal. I'm exhausted." Which is perfectly true—only I'm wired too. I need to figure out a way to come down from all the adrenaline. A hot bath might work—but I'm not ready for that, either.

"Well. I thought we were good together." Hal slides his hand down my arm, spreading his fingers wide on the small of my back, pulling me close. "I really like you." He leans in to kiss me. "Mmm, strawberry," he murmurs against my lips.

I stay with the kiss, even though it feels weird—not at all like the other night with Brandon, and that instant flare between us when he touched me. But, this is only the second time I've ever been kissed. I want to see how it stacks up to the first time.

Not well at all.

I can't get into it. I feel like a wooden doll in Hal's arms, stiff and awkward. He's moving too fast, sliding his arms around me, and grabbing my butt. His tongue invades my mouth.

Ew. Way too many germs!

I take his thick wrists in my hands and remove them from my waist, pulling away. "I liked dancing with you, Hal. We have good chemistry on the floor. But I'm sorry, I don't think this is a good idea."

"I think we have chemistry off the floor too!" He pulls his mouth down in exaggerated disappointment.

"I just don't think it is a good idea to get involved with another contestant. There are lots of pretty girls on the show. You'll meet someone who feels differently." I pat his shoulder. "Can we just be friends?"

"I guess. Want me to walk you to your room?" He cocks his head with a grin.

"What, so I can fend you off at the door? No thanks. See you tomorrow at the results show." We get new partners and start new routines tomorrow.

He sighs in exaggerated disappointment. "Okay. Friends it is."

"It's a deal." I wave goodbye, going straight to the locker room where I wash and brush my teeth, changing out of my dress into some ratty old workout wear. In the cafeteria, I join one of the tables of celebrating contestants, enjoying the laughter and camaraderie of completing the first challenge.

Done with dinner, I still don't feel ready to go up to the room —there's a good chance Alex is up there partying with Ernesto, and I just don't feel social.

I took the rhinestone pins out of my hair and peeled the brilliants off my cheeks, but I still have way too much makeup on. Oh well, nobody cares. I'll go to the gym, jog on the treadmill a little, then go to the steam room. By the time I do that, I'll be limp as a noodle and ready for bed.

The gym is practically deserted by almost nine p.m. as I push open the door. Only one woman's on the Stairmaster, and I hear the clash of dropping weights over in the weight area that's hidden by a tasteful screen.

I head straight over to the treadmill, hop on, and set it to a slow jog. I put on my headphones and turn on my Walkman, set in radio mode. After twenty minutes of Top Forty music and mindless jogging, I feel myself come down out of that jacked-up place. I'm ready to zone out in the steam room.

The hotel supplies towels, and though it's a unisex gym, I'm pretty sure I'll be the only one in there. In the women's dressing room I strip out of my gym clothes, hop in the shower for a quick rinse, and then wrap in a large bath towel. I grab a second, smaller towel to wrap around my hair.

The steam room has an automatic button and steam setting on the outside of the door. "PUSH FOR STEAM" a carved plastic notice directs.

I push the big red button and go inside.

As I hoped, it's empty, but I can't be sure it will stay that way. I spread the big towel I had wrapped around me on the tiled, shelf-like bench and lie down, covering myself with the other, much smaller towel. Steam begins to vent out of the walls.

Clouds of warm, slightly eucalyptus-smelling mist engulf me as I undo my hair. The crown-like braid has been stiffened with hairspray, and it gets stickier and stickier as the steam dampens it. My fingers tangle in the mass of strands.

"Damn." The steam is now so thick I can't see my hand in front of my face.

The door opens—I can tell by the swirl of steam escaping, and turning my head, I can see a man's muscular calves in the slightly thinner vapor close to the floor.

I freeze, one hand tangled in my hair.

"Anyone in here?" A familiar voice. Blood rushes to my face. My whole body tightens, my pulse hammering. What the heck? It's Brandon.

"Yes," I squeak, in a high-pitched voice. He can't know it's me over here.

"No worries, I'll stay over here." I see his legs disappear as he lies down on the bench along the wall opposite me.

My hand is still tangled in my hair. I have to enlist the other hand just to get it out of the mess, and let out an inadvertent yelp as I pull too hard.

"You okay?"

"Fine," I squeak, but I'm not fine. Seriously. I'm lying naked under a towel, with the man I lust for six feet away.

I should leave my hair alone, but I can't seem to. Part of my OCD, probably, but I've never been able to leave something messed up alone, be it a hangnail, a knot, or a dangling thread. I shut my eyes since I can't see through the steam anyway, trying to breathe and relax, trying to undo the knots by feel.

"I can hear you over there. Something's wrong. Are you having a health emergency?" I can tell by the change in his voice that Brandon's sitting up. "Want me to call the hotel staff? Do you need assistance?"

Dear God, he thinks I'm a little old lady having a heart attack. Anything is better than that. "It's me, Brandon. Jade."

"Jade? What's the matter?" His voice goes tight with alarm. He slides off the bench. He's approaching. One hand is stuck in my hair again but I plaster the towel tightly against me with the other.

"I'm fine. Just having a little hair situation."

He emerges suddenly out of the gouts of steam like a djinn from a bottle, looming over me, a towel wrapped around his waist. "Is your hand stuck in your hair?" Brandon's concerned expression changes to a wide grin. "That *is* a hair situation."

"The damn hairspray. The braid. The steam." I finally untangle my hand, eyes stinging with frustrated tears. "This was supposed to be relaxing."

"Let me take a look." He kneels beside my bench on the tile.

I shut my eyes. I'm too mortified by the situation to do anything but cross my arms over my breasts to hold the towel down. His fingers reach gently into the tangles, and my heart beats so loudly I'm sure he can hear it.

CHAPTER TEN

Brandon

Here I am, kneeling next to Jade with nothing on but a towel, hot steam billowing around me, trying to undo her messed-up braid.

I came to the gym to *avoid* having to run into her! I stuck my head backstage on the way here and was just in time to see that slab of a guy pull her into his arms and kiss her—though to be fair, she took his hands off and pushed him away.

Not that I have reason to care.

"Ow," she whispers, as I accidentally tug too hard.

"This is really bad. I need better light."

"Never mind. I'll just ask Alex to comb it out back at the room," she says.

I don't like the idea of Alex being able to do something I can't. Gay boys aren't the only guys with hairdressing skills. I've helped models with hair and clothing malfunctions lots of times on shoots. I trained to be an engineer—this snarl is child's play. I lean in, getting closer to see, sorting with both hands.

Jade's breath hitches, her arms tightening protectively over the towel.

She's not wearing anything under that towel. I can tell by the smooth swell of her breasts, the unbroken line of her belly, hips, and thighs disappearing into the steam. I have to press my hips against the cool tile of the bench as my groin reacts to this mental newsflash. I hope my towel is on tight enough to hold the erection down.

Her body is amazing.

Of course it is. She's a professional dancer.

Knots. Hair. I need to focus.

I gently pull the tangled skeins loose, teasing them out of the twisted mass.

Jade's eyes are closed but she breathes quickly, her cheeks pink. Sweat beads up on her skin. The pulse in her throat beats frantically.

A dove flew into my apartment window in Boston—it stunned itself and fell, landing on the fire escape. I opened the window, picked up the bird, and held it for a few minutes to make sure it was going to recover. Its tiny heart fluttered just like her pulse. Stunned. Vulnerable.

I bend closer, my breath stirring the tiny hairs near her ear. "Almost got this bit here."

Goosebumps rise on her arms in spite of the heat. She's trembling.

"This must be so uncomfortable," I whisper. "I'm almost done."

Her eyelids flutter, her lips quiver. They're so pink and full, with a curl to them. Her lashes make spiky shadows. Tiny pearls of moisture collect in the hollow of her throat.

I lift her hair gently out from under her neck and head, trailing its length down the tile as I draw my fingers through it, sorting the last of the tangles. I won't do anything more to touch her, but I want to see if she'll reach out to me.

After she ran from me the other night, the next move has to be hers.

All of her hair is hanging free now, a long stream down the side of the bench. I stiffen my fingers and rub her scalp in a gentle massage, and she moans in that breathy way she has. "Oh, Brandon. That feels so good."

"You worked hard today." I lean close and say it against her lips. Her mouth opens for me; her head tips up. I almost give in and kiss her, but *the next move has to be hers*.

Jade makes a tiny whimper of disappointment when I move away. She sits up suddenly. "Your turn."

She forgot to hold the towel on—and it falls to her waist. Her breasts are small, perfect rounds, scoops of vanilla ice cream with a pecan on top. My mouth actually waters gazing at them.

She gasps, reaches for the towel—and glances at me. Sees that I'm frozen into immobility. Though her cheeks get pinker, she doesn't cover up.

"Your turn," she repeats, deliberately.

"For what?" I can barely speak, staring at the perfect line of her breasts. They form a triangle with her navel, a delicate shell shape set in a waist so small I could spread my fingers and reach from one side to the other.

"For a massage."

This won't compute. My groin is throbbing because I'm pressed so hard against the tile. "Massage? What?"

"Your turn for a head massage, silly. Turn around and I'll do you."

"There are so many places I want to go with that sentence," I manage to say. She laughs. I hear delight in her voice, a sexual vibration. She's enjoying her effect on me.

I turn around, keeping my hands at my waist to hold my

towel on, and sit with my back against the bench. There's a rustle behind me as she sits up. Her legs slide down beside my torso to touch the floor on either side of me. My pulse pounds in my pelvis at the thought of her, naked, sitting behind me.

Her thumbs drill into the tension at the back of my neck, and my head falls forward as I groan. "Oh. Don't stop."

She laughs. Her strong little hands work my tight neck and shoulders and then back up to my head. Her fingers rub deep into my scalp, sending shivers ripping down my arms, raising the hairs on them—and then she leans forward and bites my neck.

I jerk in surprise as she latches on, sucking the side of my neck like a hot little vampire. "Are you giving me a hickey?" I yelp.

"Yes." I can hear the smile in her answer even as it's muffled by her lips on my skin. "You taste delicious. This spot right here is mine."

Okay. She made the first move.

I spin around and grab her off the bench, pulling her onto my lap. She laughs, and then we're kissing, just eating each other up. Wonderfully, her towel has fallen off entirely. I'm able to get my hand on one of those perfect breasts and roll her nipple between my fingers. She moans against my mouth. *"Ohhhh."*

I hold her close with one arm, putting her head against my shoulder, and with a bit of a wriggle, I can bend enough to get my mouth on that tender pink nipple. Talk about delicious.

"Oh!" she cries. "Oh!"

She's so responsive. Everything I do seems to turn her on. Touching her is like playing an instrument that's uniquely tuned to me. I explore her satiny skin with my mouth and hands. I can see more clearly that the automatic steam has turned off and begun to clear, and I give a happy grunt of satisfaction as I sit her back up on the edge of the bench and part her legs.

"Oh my God!" Her face is flaming, her hands tug my hair,

but I persist, prying her wide. I relish the sight before me, even as she tries to cover herself.

"Just relax. I promise you'll enjoy this," I whisper.

"Oh no—the germs..."

"Germs are a beautiful part of life. I love germs." I get down to business.

Jade tastes like peaches. In fact, that's the perfect analogy for her entire body—she has tender velvet skin, a delicate and easily bruised ripeness paired with abundant fragrance and flavor. I could explore her all day.

It doesn't take long for her to respond. She falls back on the bench. The sauna echoes with ecstatic whimpers as she finds release.

I settle back on my heels, grinning in satisfaction at how she lies there limp, knees a-sprawl, hair damp and tumbled. She looks like a Titian painting. "Told you you'd like that."

Jade sits up. Her green eyes are almost black in the dim light, hazy with satiated desire. "I had no idea what that was like..."

"That your first time?"

"For anything."

She's a virgin. That explains the fascinated, semi-horrified stare she's giving my equipment now that my towel has fallen off. "Um—do you have a condom?" she asks with forced sophistication, pushing a handful of hair out of her face as she covers herself with one of the damp towels.

"Not on me, no." Definitely not going to have her first time be on hard tile in the sauna room of the gym. I'll have to plan the whole thing so that it's a truly memorable experience. I realize what I'm thinking and shake my head. This encounter was totally random...but now I'm going to take it to the next level?

"It's your turn. Get up on the bench," she says.

"It's okay. That's enough for tonight." I reach for my towel.

Jade frowns. "Oh no. You got me all crazy. Now I'm going to make you crazy, too."

My erection throbs, casting a solid vote for letting her do her worst. "I'm fine," I lie.

She grabs my nipple and twists, and I can't decide if it's good or painful. "On the bench, Mister Boss Man Producer. You're going to like this."

Girl's got a touch of the dominatrix going on. I *do* like it. I get up onto the bench and she kneels between my thighs, pushing them as wide as I did hers. I resist an urge to pull away, to shut down—but she needs to feel in charge. I've never felt so vulnerable, so exposed—but it's damn sexy too.

"Like what you see?" I say to the crown of Jade's head as she studies my anatomy. My heart is roaring in my ears.

"Oh, yes," she says seriously. She circles me with her hand and then licks me deliberately. "Mm. Tastes good, too."

My erection jumps and strains in her hand and I groan. She takes me in her mouth and goes to work. Within minutes I'm bucking out of control, hitting my head on the tiled wall I come so hard. She stays with it all the way to the end, like there's nothing she won't do for me.

"Holy shit." I tip over to the side, sweating, panting, wrung out like I ran a mile in five. "Jade. That was insane."

Jade dabs her lips on her towel and stands up. She's magnificent naked. I stare at her perfect, lithe body so I can remember it always.

"Told you you'd like it." Jade smiles as she catches my eye, enjoying throwing my words back at me. She picks up a towel, wraps it around herself, and walks out the door.

"Jade!" But by the time I get my towel on and follow, she's disappeared.

CHAPTER ELEVEN

Jade

THE NEXT DAY I PULL Ernesto Barza as a partner for hip-hop. He grins with straight, perfectly white teeth. "Good. I want to see what you got, little girl."

"Not so much littler than you."

Ernesto is actually the perfect height to partner me at about five ten, and his dark good looks are a nice foil for mine. Last night, when I finally got back to the room, I was grateful to find that he and Alex had gone somewhere else.

I'm still feeling kind of aglow from the encounter with Brandon in the sauna last night, though still not at all sure how to face him if we run into each other today. I hid in the women's locker room and changed after I heard him leave the sauna last night.

I don't know where this relationship is going and don't want to have to think about it, either. Hiding had seemed like a perfectly legitimate short-term solution.

Whenever I remember those intense moments with him, my heart rate spikes. Holy crap. I can't believe we did what we did.

And in the steam room, where anyone could have walked in on us! And what he did with his mouth...And what I did with mine...and the germs involved!

I waited for the familiar germ horror to return and steal the good feelings last night, but it never happened. I hopped into the gym shower and washed briskly, feeling amazing. Alex had gone elsewhere, and our suite was mercifully empty. I slept like the proverbial log.

"How are you at hip-hop?" Ernesto asks, hands on hips. His lean, chiseled body, every muscle perfectly defined, reminds me of a well-made sword.

"One of my better modalities." He scans me up and down doubtfully. I'm wearing my usual pale pink ballet gear and little leather flats. "Oh ye of little faith."

Our coach and choreographer for the day arrives, a muscular black man wearing nylon warm-up pants, a net shirt, and so many tattoos that his skin looks like fabric. He claps his hands like a pistol shot and we both jump.

"Ernesto and Jade. I'm Saladin. You're mine today, and you're going to dance like you've never danced before. I want to see you both move." He walks over to a boom box against one mirrored wall. "Let's see what you've got."

He pushes Play, and MC Hammer's *U Can't Touch This* blares from the box.

I can't help grinning. The song's been out a while, but it's so catchy and fun—and of course, I've watched the music video on MTV and practiced many of the same rapid knee and elbow moves as the dancers on the video. I bust into some of that as Ernesto does the same.

Ernesto drops for some ground work while I stay up high doing kicks and jumps. Instinctively we swivel to face each other. The impromptu dance becomes a conversation—I go low, you go high. I go left, you go right—but always, we match each other in rhythm, speed and intensity.

The moment that Ernesto believes in me and knows I'm his equal breaks across his face in a compelling grin, and I smile back. It's an amazing feeling to be perfectly in sync with a partner this strong.

Saladin cuts the music and claps his hands again, bringing us to face him. "Sweet. You're both better than average. I've got some choreography for you, but I liked what just happened there, how you played off each other. The dances that steal the show tell a story—and the oldest story in the world, the story of love, that's what will light up the audience and move them to dial their phones."

What Saladin's saying makes sense to me. We both draw closer to him, nodding. "I didn't pre-work any choreography for this piece. I wanted to see what level you two would bring to the floor, and how you'd look together and play off each other. I like what I see. We're going to use this song, but we're going to infuse it with a story. Jade, you're the innocent, untouched virgin from a good home—'he can't touch this.' Ernesto, you're gonna be the bad boy from the wrong side of the tracks who wants to." My heart thuds in response to this. How did Saladin read me as the 'good girl virgin' so well? Was it the pink outfit?

This feels way too close to home.

"I think I could be a bad girl going after nice Catholic boy Ernesto," I say boldly. "Put me in some tight leathers. I can pull it off."

Both of them stare at me. Ernesto folds his arms, frowning. "Do I look like a nice Catholic boy?"

"It won't play." Saladin's eyes are so dark I can't see his pupils. "You are what you are. Embrace it. Own it. Work it, sweet little virgin." My cheeks flame, and I want to drop through the floor. "Let me demonstrate some choreography you two may not have seen."

Saladin moves like mercury, boneless and smooth, rippling himself, twisting his arms around each other in an optical illusion of a knot. We spend several hours mastering the unique subroutines he wants us to integrate into our number, finally storyboarding the routine on a long piece of butcher paper on the floor.

By four p.m., we have the piece roughed out and it's time to prep for the results show from the day before.

"Grab something to eat, take a shower, then get down to Wardrobe," Saladin tells us. "I'll see you bright and early for more practice tomorrow morning. You two are going to knock it out of the park." He allows himself a little smile. "And it wouldn't be a bad idea for you two to get out on the dance floor in your spare time. Keep working the chemistry."

We walk down the hall. Ernesto slings an arm around my shoulders. It feels hot, sticky, and germy. I wish he would take it off, but I don't say anything because we've become friends through the intense day of working together. "You've got more goin' on than I gave you credit for," he says. "I think we're going to kill it tomorrow."

"If we don't get killed tonight." I'm thinking of yesterday's foxtrot with Hal. "I'm sorry, I was too distracted to pay much attention to your performance yesterday. How do you think you did?"

"Okay. It was the cha-cha with that hot brunette, Sally. She's better than me."

"I was with Hal and his foxtrot was better than mine, too. So let's both hope."

"Deal." He takes his arm off my shoulder, but hooks my pinkie finger in his. Guy's definitely a toucher, and I'm not. "Want to party with me and Alex later?"

"Uh...I don't know. Depends on what you mean by that."

He grins and winks at me. "I think you can imagine."

What is he saying? My brain fritzes out and I pretend I didn't hear that. We reach the dining area and Alex, clearly waiting for us, waves from a table. We go through the cafeteria-style line and sit down with him.

"Holding pinkies? Do I need to be jealous, Hot Stuff?" he asks Ernesto.

"Only if you want to be," Ernesto says, and plants a big one on Alex's lips.

I clean my hands with hand sanitizer and address my mound of pasta while they kiss. I'm uncomfortable with public displays of affection, no matter what the orientation of the people involved. Forking up my pasta, I wonder why it bothers me to have Ernesto put an arm over my shoulders or hook my pinkie with his, but not have Brandon touch my actual... I can't even complete the thought without blushing.

"So, little girl here and I are gonna steal the show tomorrow." Ernesto cuts into the slab of salmon on his plate. "She's got moves. I asked her if she wanted to party with us later tonight."

"Sorry, Ernesto. Not only am I sure your kind of partying isn't my thing, I need my beauty sleep for tomorrow... and if I'm booted off the show tonight, I'll want to lick my wounds in private."

"Good thing, too, because I'm not into sharing." Alex nips his partner's ear.

I finish my pasta, say my goodbyes, and head to Wardrobe. *Oh, boy.* Ernesto clearly swings either way and from the chandelier if that's available, while I'm still trying to figure out how to kiss without wanting to use mouthwash after!

Except with Brandon. Everything's good with Brandon. I can't help smiling at how good.

CHAPTER TWELVE

Brandon

THERE'S BEEN SO MUCH TO do today I've hardly had time to grab a bite to eat—but I can't stop my mind from flashing repeatedly to that unreal encounter with Jade in the sauna room.

Did it really happen? I wouldn't believe it if the hickey on my neck, a scarlet mark I've hidden with a shirt and tie, didn't provide proof. It makes me grin every time I think of her biting my neck like that—talk about a surprise first move.

"You're in a good mood, Boss," Kerry tells me.

"Slept well, for once." I'm glad Stu is filming on the floor and can't give me shit—we've partied enough together over the years that he'd be able to guess why I'm feeling a hell of a lot better about life today.

Phone calls, money management, and other crises temporarily under control, I head down to the film editing room.

We've got video piped into the editing room from all the studio areas where couples are practicing.

"I'd like to get a look at the different pairings for today," I tell

Brad, one of the video editors. He nods and pulls up a live feed channel from each of the warren of practice rooms.

Jade's with Ernesto Barza, that kid who blew us away at the tryouts with his very original flamenco-breakdance mishmash piece. From the looks of it, the dude does mean hip-hop. I sit back, grinning with relief, as I see that that Jade can, too.

In her usual pretty-girl pink, Jade's breaking like mad, improvising some bold moves to MC Hammer's *U Can't Touch This*. Under the watchful eye of Saladin, one of the show's best choreographers, these two are going to burn up their routine.

Good.

The hours fly by, and soon it's time to film the results show.

I keep myself from checking the list of who made the cut to the next level by leaving the envelope sealed and sending it by intern to Kate for the announcement.

I don't want to know ahead of time, and I don't want to think too much about why.

It's been a long, hot day by that time. I haul off the tie and unbutton my collar as I sit down with Alan in the little cockpit area below the stage reserved for us. I munch a hot dog that Clay from UCLA brings me from the cafeteria. We aren't supposed to eat in the theater, but I dare anyone to call me on it.

The audience begins filing in. I stand and turn to see how the seats are filling up. We had a packed house for the first show.

One of the overhead lights picks out Pearl's silver-blonde hair like a spot is set right on her—she's always seemed to emanate a glow.

She's holding hands with her husband. The guy is huge, muscles packing his suit like it's filled with boulders. He wears a long black ponytail and scars on his face. She's married to a guy who looks like a Native American WWF wrestler turned mob enforcer, but the way he settles her in her seat tells me everything I need to know about their relationship.

Following them is their mother, a good-looking woman with Jade's dark auburn hair, streaked with ribbons of gray. Ruby, the redheaded oldest sister, enters the aisle holding a little boy's hand, followed by her husband Rafe. Ruby seems to be looking for someone, scanning the crowd. She spots me and smiles, gesturing for me to join them. Rafe looks over and waves too, a big grin splitting his face.

I might as well get this over with.

"Be right back," I tell the director, and head up the aisle.

I gave Jade's family a premium row of seats, right in the middle and only a couple of rows back, so it's a short walk.

"Hey, Rafe." I shake hands with the tall, blue-eyed sailor tycoon who gave me the third degree about taking Pearl out back in the day. I gesture to the little boy. "Who's this young man?"

"Peter McCallum," the tot pipes up loudly.

Ruby laughs, leaning over to give me an air kiss. "Brandon, thanks so much for the tickets. We're so excited to be here."

On the other side of Ruby, Pearl stands up with her husband. The guy shakes my hand and it hurts. "I'm Magnus. Thanks for the perk." He claps me on the back so hard my teeth rattle.

"My pleasure." My gaze finds Pearl's, and she smiles. *God, she's beautiful.* She looks at my neck and smiles bigger. Damn, I forgot about the hickey and took my tie off. Thank God she doesn't know who put it there.

"It's great to see you again. We really appreciate this." Pearl touches my shoulders for an awkward triangular hug and an air kiss that doesn't touch my cheek. "We haven't told Jade we're here. We want to surprise her after the show."

"I'm sure she'll be thrilled." I switch gears and give my full attention to Jade's mother. "Mrs. Michaels. I'm Brandon Forbes. Such a pleasure to meet you. I see where the girls get their good looks."

"Oh, thank you." Maggie Michaels flaps a hand dismissively,

smiling, and lets me kiss her cheek. "I can't wait to see Jade dance!"

"Well, that's not happening tonight." I explain the format of the show, and that they'll see her dance live tomorrow. "I understand if you can't stay for the duration of the show, because we run for ten days of filming—or until she gets eliminated, whichever comes first."

"She won't be eliminated," Mrs. Michaels says flatly. "Jade wants this. And what Jade wants, Jade gets."

"I hope you're right," I smile. "Seems like all the Michaels women might be cut from that cloth." Both Rafe and Magnus nod vigorously, and the women laugh.

The lights dim.

"I gotta go back. Enjoy the show." I raise a hand and trot down the aisle to my seat. Settling in as the lights dim and the contestants file out on stage, I mentally probe how I'm feeling about Pearl.

Not bad. I'm finally okay with it. I think. I hope.

She's still one of the most beautiful women in the world, and I appreciate that—but there's no chemistry between us—not the slightest fizzle. All that energy's crackling in the air between her and her husband.

Not to mention, Magnus could pound me into the ground like a tent stake with just one fist if I so much as looked at her.

Which I'm no longer interested in doing.

It's Jade I'm searching the stage for.

Jade comes out onstage, holding hands with Hal the Barn Door. They stand close together in the milling herd of contestants.

Kate does the intro and sets up the tension for the results show, ushering all the contestants to a temporary bleacher on the side where our cameras can mine their faces for stress and detail while waiting.

Meanwhile, another professional troupe comes out and performs an acrobatic hip-hop routine ending in some crazy Cirque du Soleil human pyramid shit.

The crowd loves it.

I'm itchy in my shirt, wishing I could take a shower and cool off, but there's no time as Kate counts down the results. Two couples will be leaving us tonight, and the format drags out the agony with highlight recaps of the contestants.

Jade's family screams and whoops like crazy as the crew runs the clip of her Dirty Dancing-style lift with Slab O' Beef. I can see on the director's monitor that he's had the cameras pan back to the source of the noise.

Ruby, Rafe, and little Peter are holding up a big cardboard sign reading *Way To Go, Jade!*

Another camera zooms in on Jade in the stands. Her eyes are huge and welling with tears, both hands over her mouth in amazed happiness as she gazes at her family in the audience.

I feel a crazy-good tightness in my chest. Don't know what it is. Don't want to know.

But I did something that put that happiness on her face, and I like it.

Finally, Kate announces the bottom eight. Jade and Hal are not in the sad crew that has to stand in a half-moon of shame on the stage while Kate prolongs the agony and the team runs clips of her interviews with each of them, then the judges' hammer falls.

Four return to the bleachers, and four do a weepy goodbye dance as confetti falls around them like rain. A few minutes into it the rest of the group surges down from the stands to hug them and wish the losers well.

Attrition over the next ten days will knock that group off one by one until only two remain. I really hope one of them is Jade.

I help the director pack up his crap and we get ready to head to the film review room as Jade hops off the stage in that rosy dress with the sparkles, running past me up the aisle to her family.

I turn to watch, the monitor in my arms, as she throws herself into her mother's arms. Her sisters surround her, and the whole family is a blur of motion and happiness.

"Let's get back to the edits," Alan says. Lugging the monitor, I follow him.

What would it be like to belong to a family like that? Mine is a tense group of two—me and my mother, the "legendary" Melissa. We hardly hug, let alone jump up and down for joy. But I made that joy happen for Jade today, and along the way a little of it rubbed off on me.

CHAPTER THIRTEEN

Jade

I CAN HARDLY BELIEVE THAT MY entire family is here. Mom's face is shiny with tears, my little nephew Peter has his arms around my waist, and Ruby and Pearl are hugging me too as Rafe and Magnus smile and look on.

"You look like the Sugarplum Fairy in this getup," Mom says. "I'm so glad you made it to the next round! How am I going to handle ten more days of this?"

"I don't know, Mom, I'm having trouble too—but you guys coming is going to make it much better, no matter what. I can't believe how special it is for us all to be in one place. How did you get here? To this? Rafe, did you set this up? Cuz if so, good job." Rafe is a zillionaire who makes everything look easy. Bringing the family out to LA in the Learjet is just the great kind of thing he'd do.

"Well, not quite." Rafe brushes a bit of lint off his black dress shirt. "I did have the jet round everyone up, but I think you owe thanks to Pearl. She called that producer, Brandon Forbes, and he sent tickets for all of us. Great seats, too."

I turn to Pearl as my heart sinks. That phrase is one of those clichés that's just the right way to describe the sensation I'm feeling, a sort of dropping, hollow tightness that begins in my chest and ends in my stomach.

"Pearl?" I whisper. "You called Brandon? I mean, Mr. Forbes?"

Pearl fiddles with the tassels on her fancy Coach bag. "I did. He's an old friend. I called him to see if you'd made it onto the show. He offered the tickets to us himself."

"I know what kind of 'friend' of yours he was," I say through clenched teeth. "How great of him to do this for *you*." I turn my back and give Mom and Ruby another hug. "Well, I'm sure glad to see you! Have you eaten? We have a great cafeteria."

I manage not to address Pearl the rest of the evening. She doesn't seem to notice, bantering with everyone else.

While we're sitting in the caf, one of the cameramen spots Pearl—that skinny guy with the gauged ears—Stu—who filmed Alex and me in the street. He runs over carrying his equipment, followed by Kate, the emcee. Of course, it's Pearl they want to talk to.

"Hi, Pearl. Welcome to *Dance, Dance, Dance!* What a great outfit, you look beautiful!" Kate gushes. Pearl does look great, wearing a pantsuit in gray silk, a wide leather belt cinching her waist. Her shimmery silver-blonde hair brushes her shoulders like tinsel.

"Thanks, but this is my sister Jade's special day." Pearl looks right at me. "I'm just here to support her."

Kate ignores that. "So what's it like for you to have your little sister dancing on national TV?"

Pearl's still looking me in the eyes. I can't seem to look away. "I'm just so proud of Jade. She's so talented and works amazingly hard. America's not going to believe what she can do."

Pearl sounds sincere. Maybe she is sincere. But really?

Calling Brandon to get special favors for the show? I'm not sure who I want to kill more, Pearl or Brandon.

"There you have it, folks, supermodel Pearl Michaels is here to support her sister!" The bright light, camera and mic swing to my face next.

I'm no dummy. I can't let my conflicted feelings show. I switch on a smile.

"I'm so thrilled the family could make it out to watch the filming!" I clasp my hands together. "My family's the best. Meet my sister Ruby." I introduce the whole family on camera. They get their sound bite, and finally move on.

After dinner, tiredness from the day creeps in, gray around the edges of my vision. "Where are you guys staying?" I ask Mom.

"We have rooms here at the hotel." Rafe's sitting beside Ruby, one big hand on the back of her neck, massaging, as she leans against him. I thought it was pretty nuts when Ruby married him as a freshman in college, but it sure worked out great. Three-year-old Peter, intent on a little pile of blocks next to his plate, is the perfect addition to their family. As if reading my mind, Ruby smiles at me.

"We've got some exciting news to share. We're having another baby." Ruby pats her tummy fondly. "I'm three months along, so it's safe to tell people."

"Oh, that's so great! I'm so happy for you!" I glance at Peter. "You're going to have a little sister or brother, buddy."

"Yeah." He leans against Ruby's side. "I want to play with him."

We all laugh.

Magnus, from across the table, gives Pearl's hand a tug. "We're bushed. Need to get to our room for some shut-eye. We'll see you tomorrow night after the show, Jade. Break a leg!"

"I've never liked that saying," I reply, and he laughs. We all say goodbye. I turn back to Mom as they leave. "I'd love to visit more, but Ernesto and I have a big day of practice and then performance tomorrow. Want me to walk you to your room so I know where it is?"

"No, that's fine, dear. I'm staying in a two-bedroom suite with Rafe and Ruby. We'll be fine." She tells me the suite number and leans over to kiss me. "You freaked me out, sneaking off like that. I was the one who asked Ruby and Pearl to try to find you."

"I'm sorry. I did call and leave you a message...but I couldn't stand to have anyone try to talk me out of the audition. And then, if I didn't make it..." I hug Mom, breathing in her familiar scent, that of coconut and jasmine. She has a friend from St. Thomas mail her the oil she uses on her skin, and it's a potent reminder of those warm, lazy childhood days in the Virgin Islands. "I'm sorry if I worried you. I just wish Dad was here with all of us."

"Me, too, darling. But tell me what you're doing next time." Mom waggles a finger. "You may be twenty, but I'm still your mom."

"Who could forget that?" I hug her again, and kiss and hug Ruby, Peter, and Rafe too. "If you see Brandon, tell him thanks for me, will you?" It's the right thing to say.

"You can tell him yourself." Rafe points.

I turn. Brandon is entering the door of the cafeteria area. Wearing a wine-colored dress shirt, no tie, and dark slacks, he looks like he could be modeling menswear.

It takes a long minute, but I remember that I'm mad at him.

Rafe waves for him to approach. He does, weaving among the tables like a matador.

"How's the food tonight?" He addresses Rafe.

"Not bad, not bad at all. Jade was just saying how she wanted to thank you for the tickets," Rafe prompted.

"Yes, so kind of you to do that for Pearl," I emphasize her name.

"And let's not forget how nice it was for Pearl to call me, worried about you. She's a good big sister." Brandon's brows draw together, registering that I'm not happy.

Rather: I'm happy that the family's here, but I'm not happy he brought them here because of Pearl.

Or something like that.

I'm confused.

"Well, thanks. It was nice of you," I say, finally.

"It sure was!" Ruby smiles at Brandon. She always says the right thing—unlike me, the freaky, awkward Michaels sister. "And to make it perfect, we got rooms here and can eat here, too. So convenient. We're going to the zoo and to do some sightseeing tomorrow—we're making this into a real family vacation. Thanks again."

"Well, like I said, I have to get to bed early." I brush a few crumbs off my Sugarplum Fairy dress. "I hope it's okay to return this to Costume tomorrow?" I ask Brandon.

"Sure. Can I have a word?" Brandon takes my arm. I wave back at the family and we walk toward the entrance. As soon as decently possible, I tweak my arm out of his grasp.

This is the first time I've noticed that icky human-contact feeling all day, and I've hardly thought about germs today either. Maybe this contest is working to get me over the phobia? But why does Brandon's touch activate that feeling sometimes, and not others?

Definitely not others. I think of the sauna again.

I stop in the hall outside the cafeteria. "Listen, Brandon, I'm really tired. I've danced all day and had a stressful evening. I really do need to get back to my room and get some rest."

"Okay. I'll just walk you to your room, and we can talk on the way."

"Why?"

He swings to fully face me, and those gold-green eyes seem to blaze. "You know why."

"No, I don't know why." I fold my arms over my chest. The rhinestones on the bodice scratch my skin. "Just like I don't know why you got the tickets for Pearl."

"No good deed goes unpunished!" Brandon throws his hands up. "I just thought it would be nice for you to have your family come support you!"

I start walking, feeling guilty, but surly now, too. I can't explain my fear that he made the gesture for Pearl, not me, without being a whole lot more vulnerable than I'm willing to be right now. "It was nice of you to send the tickets. I mean that sincerely. Thanks."

I try to say it in a tone that conveys I mean it. I'm so mad at myself right now—I really don't like how I'm being mean.

To Brandon. To Pearl.

The honest to God truth is, I'm *jealous*. I can hardly bear to admit it. Even to myself.

We reach the elevator and it opens promptly. We get on, standing side by side, facing the doors. His nearness vibrates like an electric field next to me.

Brandon hits the STOP button on the elevator after a moment. "Where'd you run off to last night?" He is still facing forward, not looking at me, and I'm so fixated on the tickets and the Pearl issue that I'm taken by surprise. Color floods my face as I remember last night.

The sauna. And that I hid, after.

"I just went to the locker room and changed. When I left, you were gone." Perfectly true, to a degree.

"It felt like you were running away from me." He's still not looking at me. "I didn't like you disappearing like that. It felt... like you were... uncomfortable with me. With what we did."

"I was. I am. I've never done anything like that before. I don't know how I'm supposed to act." It's easier to talk without looking at him, standing side by side like wooden soldiers in the box of the elevator. "It was so—random."

His mouth twitches up. "Yeah. And yet—I can't stop thinking about it."

My face heats. "Me too."

He finally turns to me, slowly, as if to keep from spooking me. A big cat stalks prey with the kind of deliberateness with which he slides his warm hands up the jeweled netting on my arms, all the way to my neck. My pulse hammers as he takes just one step closer, and that magnetism between us intensifies, lifting every tiny hair on my body. We're separated by mere inches. Slowly, so slowly, his mouth drifts down to mine.

I fall against him as my knees go instantly soft, and like two powerful magnets, we collide. My mouth opens to his and he angles my head with his hands for better access.

Warm pulsing redness behind my closed eyes. Swirling. Spinning. Taking. Giving.

His hands roam, skimming my edges. My hands clutch his shoulders. I'll fall over if I don't hang on.

"Jade," he whispers against my mouth. "You taste so good. You feel so good. I can't get enough of you."

I have no words for how he tastes, how he feels. All rational thoughts cease as I press tight to him. My arms twine around his neck, pulling him closer, as we dive into the kiss again.

I hate the clothing between us, the barriers, the misunderstandings. There must be a way through all that and I'm desperate to find it—but I have no words. Words seem to mess it up even more. But when we touch—it all works.

Maybe that's the answer.

He pushes me against the wall of the elevator, sliding his hands up to clasp my waist, squeezing. "I love this ribbon. I love watching this ribbon when you dance."

He's standing between my spread legs, the froth of pale pink tulle skirt bunched between us. I can feel myself melting, wanting him.

Oh, if he could just unzip those tailored pants and slide into me...I'm ready for it. I want it. I tug at his belt buckle and he's so busy kissing me, his hands spanning my waist, that he doesn't notice until I get the buckle of his belt and the top button of his pants undone and I'm rubbing my hand over the thick ridge there.

He groans, pulls back. He's withdrawing. "No. Your first time —it's going to be amazing. Not here."

"How do you know it's my first time?" I tug at his belt again, impatient, burning. Damn it, I want this. He smiles down at me and those green-gold eyes seem to glow.

"You're kidding, right?"

He knows.

I sigh, and clasp the corners of his richly colored collar and set my lips on the warm triangle of skin where the buttons of his shirt begin.

"Mine," I growl, and kiss him there, where his pulse pounds beneath my lips. God, he tastes good, and smells good too.

"No biting me," he chuckles. "I had to wear a tie today, and I think Pearl saw the mark on my neck."

The mention of Pearl freezes me for a long moment. I step back out of his arms.

I have to say something, put my fear into words. "What is going on here, Brandon? Is this—what we're doing—about her? Am I just... some sort of consolation prize since she chose Magnus, not you?"

Brandon draws himself taller. He straightens his shirt and takes a step back even further from me. His face shuts down, going remote and hard-edged. The warm color of his eyes cools to brass.

"I don't know what this is," he says. "But it's not about Pearl."

He turns away and hits the STOP button again. We trundle on, and he gets off at his floor without looking back or acknowledging me.

I'm too tired and numb to cry when I finally get into the shower and try to figure out how to untangle my elaborately braided hair alone.

CHAPTER FOURTEEN

Jade

Saladin is wearing an open leather vest and a pair of baggy satin pants at practice the next morning. He looks more than ever like a djinn.

"Ready?" he says. "Let's do some warm-up. We'll just dance freestyle and do stretches."

He stands in front of us facing the mirrored wall. As the music comes on, a mix of hip-hop, R & B and disco, we get down and funky. I learn just watching Saladin. He shows me how far I can grow. An hour later, smiling, hot, loose in the joints and muscles, we're ready to get back to our routine.

Saladin rolls out the butcher paper outline. "Take a look. Let's see what you remember."

He cues the music. We get started, and pretty soon we're back to where we were the day before.

Ernesto really is a sexy guy, and the way he moves—crisp, but somehow lingering, like there's an echo in the air behind him— infuses our "story" with a passionate burn, every appearance of real longing. I feel that longing between my thighs, along my nerve endings, and it makes me think of Brandon more than I have room or time for.

We have some spectacular screw-ups: the time I'm supposed to slide down his back and land in a roll, and instead just land on my tailbone with a bone-jarring thud. The time Ernesto's supposed to cartwheel over me and instead, lands his hand right on my hip, mashing me into the unforgiving floor. The time our heads crack together as we leap toward each other.

"You kids are going to be sore tomorrow," Saladin tells us at the end of the day, "but remember—today's the day that matters. Tomorrow is just the results show and new partners, a whole day to get going on your next routine. So give it all you have tonight." The choreographer puts his ropy, tattooed arms around us and pulls us in for a hug. Our foreheads touch in a sweaty, smelly, warm and wonderful bond. "Make me proud."

I walk away toward Wardrobe blinking tears out of my eyes, amazed that I still don't need to sanitize after all that sweaty contact.

"I wish he was our choreographer for all the pieces," Ernesto says as we walk down the hall. "He's a master."

"Me too."

"And I wish you were my partner every day, too."

"Ah, you're just saying that."

Ernesto slings his arm over me in that way he has, skimming my arm with his fingertips. This time, I don't like it—that icky human contact feeling again, for the first time today. "We have some mean chemistry. I could make it good for you," he says.

I know what he's talking about. "Ernesto. Damn it. I'm not into you that way." I'm getting tired of having to have this conversation with every randomly assigned partner.

We pause in the dimly lit hall. The overhead fluorescent flickers over us, bathing us in chilly grayish light—but even then, he's attractive with his large brown eyes, coppery-gold skin, full lips and that body that defies description. "Just sayin.' The story we're telling in the dance works for me."

"I agree that it works. *On stage.* We'll work it hard. But even if I *did* like you that way, which I don't, Alex is my friend. And like he told you last night, he's not into sharing."

"Too bad. I'm not ready to settle down, and Alex is going to have to deal."

"Well, be nice, will you?" I reach over and touch his arm. "Please don't hurt him."

"Can't help it. I'm a heartbreaker."

I sock him in the shoulder for that.

We reach the costuming area and get outfitted. There's just time to go to the cafeteria, wolf down a little food, shower, and get ready.

It's show time.

Brandon

I'm going to watch the action tonight from the film booth with Brad, the producer. I send Tad from Yale to be the director's helper in the pit. I sit down in front of the bank of camera monitors with the fifth cup of coffee of the day and the agenda for the night. Tonight, I want to keep an eye on the big picture of the show.

At least, that's what I tell myself.

The tight, achy feeling in my chest tells me something else might be going on—something like getting more distance from Jade and her family. I really need to shut this thing between us down. The last thing I need is a complication like a relationship with someone like Jade—it wouldn't be a quick bang in the elevator—and I won't get attached to another Michaels girl.

God forbid. It took me four years to get over the last one.

Melissa's biopsy went smoothly, according to our phone call today. Now we have to wait on the results.

She's still on me about finding her some talent from this crop of dancers, and that led to my proposal that I run a separate talent agency. The idea's been rattling around in my head for a while, but it really became clear today as I reviewed the dailies and interviews. I've identified five, possibly six dancers, all with that extra something that translates into screen magnetism. Jade is one of them.

"I can keep boosting you print models as I come across them," I tell Melissa. "But I want to run my own talent agency. The music video industry is taking off here in LA, and I'm in an ideal position to spot dance and acting talent. You have your niche, and this can be mine."

The distance between LA and Boston hisses on the phone line. I wait for the frosty, biting rebuttal.

"All right," Mom says abruptly. "I'm at a stage in my life when I want to... take some time off. Smell the roses and the like. So that's fine—let's move ahead with an agency separation."

A possible cancer diagnosis is giving Mom a new set of priorities. I get it. "Thanks for not giving me shit about this, Mom."

"Far from it, son. But as you know, I already got the talent aspect of The Melissa Agency started. My former photographer, Chad Wicke, is heading it up. If you like, I'll hand him and the portfolio over to you. You can build the new agency with him. The man's got an uncanny eye for seeing past the surface with some of these performers."

"Chad Wicke! Seriously, you'd let him go?" Chad's one of Mom's secret weapons. That fashionista photographer has a way of pulling amazing things out of models.

"He wants to get out from behind the camera and do more hands-on development work. He's been enjoying putting together our portfolios on the dance and acting talent. I'll turn that whole operation over to you."

"Thanks, Mom. I think this is a good move for us." I wish she was closer so I could hug her and read her face, make sure this is really okay with her. "I appreciate your confidence in me." The Michaels family, hugging and jumping, flashes into my mind. I wonder if I could ever hug and rejoice over a victory like that with Mom. Maybe it's time I tried to find a way to make that kind of thing happen. "I love you, Mom."

A surprised silence on her end, then I hear her sniff. Her voice is wobbly. "I love you too, son. I'll call you as soon as I hear the biopsy results." She hangs up softly.

That's my mom. Classy. Understated. Loving in her way.

The lights are coming up on the stage and I refocus on the night's lineup. Jade and Ernesto are fourth in line of the six couples performing—not that I'm focusing on them.

The night's performances take it up a notch from the previous ones, no question. The contestants are getting more confident, learning the ropes and the routine of the show. They know what to expect now, and that shapes the way they throw themselves into the performances. There's already been one standing ovation by the time Jade and Ernesto take the stage to that MC Hammer song.

Wardrobe outfitted them according to the theme of the "story" they tell through the dance. Ernesto wears split-kneed jeans, boots, and a chain-laden leather jacket over a tight net shirt, the picture of a bad boy. Jade wears a short, fluffy white confirmation-style dress. She's made it her own by tying that black ribbon around her waist. Her hair is in two braids, and she looks like a schoolgirl—until she spins, and the audience can see that the whole back of the dress is bare, ending just above her perfect butt.

The two put on a riveting performance: a blend of styles,

trademark Saladin choreography that includes hip-hop, pop and lock and some mean acrobatic breakdancing—and it's not just moves. The piece tells a tale of forbidden love and temptation.

Every hair on my body rises at the sensuality and passion of the performance—and something else rises too, mercifully hidden by the desk. The routine ends with a spotlight on the couple as Ernesto, on his knees, embraces Jade's tiny waist, entreating, pulling her down—and she slowly leans over. They kiss.

It looks like a real kiss.

"Zoom in with camera three," I snap at Brad. The camera's merciless eye flies in to spy on the lovers.

Yes, their lips are touching.

Jade's eyes are closed, her cheeks flushed from exertion. There's a dew of moisture on her skin. She's luscious as the peach she reminds me of. Ernesto's dark and dangerous good looks set her off even more—and that jerk's hands are sliding down her hips, pulling her into him even more.

I'm pretty sure this whole section wasn't part of the choreography.

The audience is standing and applauding. A rose whacks Ernesto in the back, and he finally lets go of Jade and stands, turning with an insouciant grin and a flourishing bow. Jade curtsies.

I want to kill that bastard for taking advantage of Jade to cop a feel and a kiss during a performance on national TV. Hopefully he'll get voted off tonight. But it's not likely, with that performance. The girls are going nuts for him, if the screams of "Ernesto!" are anything to go by.

"Camera four on the audience, middle section," I direct. The camera's eye zooms in on the Michaels family, yelling and jumping. Jade's mom Maggie is openly crying as the sisters hug, the husbands clap, and Peter waves the sign.

Kate the emcee reminds the audience of Jade and Ernesto's numbers for voting, and ushers them offstage.

Ernesto is still holding Jade's hand.

Damn it.

But I made my choice in the elevator. I walked away. She's not mine to claim—or protect.

The rest of the show passes in a blur: the final two performances, the appeals at the end. During the highlight recaps from each performance, Brad runs a clip of Jade and Ernesto cartwheeling over each other, not the kiss at the end.

Good thing, too. I don't think I could stand to watch that again.

Jade

I barely make it backstage before I'm pulling the tiny vial of hand sanitizer out of my waistband and rubbing my hands briskly thirteen times, and then wiping my lips with another dot of it. Ernesto spots this. "What the hell? Hand sanitizer on your mouth, really?"

"Germs," I say. "That kiss wasn't in the choreography."

"It went along with the story, and I didn't see you fighting it," Ernesto grins. "We killed it tonight. Even better than the practice."

"I agree." But I still want to get distance from him.

I go to stand beside Alex. He's dressed in black ballet tights, no shirt, and looks amazing. He performed second in the lineup with that girl Selina, who's terrific and is shaping up as one of the top female talents of the show. They earned the first standing ovation of the evening.

Alex turns his back on me.

I touch his shoulder. "Alex."

He twitches my hand away and walks off without looking at me. I swing back to Ernesto, who winks and shrugs.

There's no time for more communication as they call us out for the final appeal for votes, and we all bow, and confetti and balloons fall as we break out into some improv moves and a great cut of music ends the show for the night.

I change out of my "confirmation" dress and into some sweats backstage, and meet the family at the cafeteria for dinner, as we planned the day before. Little Peter runs across the dining room to hug me.

"Your dress was so pretty, Auntie," he says. With all that's going on, I've hardly had time to think about Ruby's pregnancy, but looking up at my smiling sister, I'm so happy for them.

"Thanks, buddy." I sit down with the group, registering that Pearl isn't there though Magnus is already seated, digging into a mounded plate of meat and vegetables.

"You and that Ernesto guy were smokin' hot," Ruby says. "Great performance."

"Yeah, you've got our votes," Rafe says.

"I don't know about that kiss," Magnus rumbles beside me. "That didn't look like part of the program."

"It wasn't. Ernesto—he got swept away by the moment, I guess, and I didn't have much choice but to go along." I can feel how hot my cheeks are. "How was everyone's day? Where's Pearl?"

"She went up to bed right after the show," Magnus says. "She wasn't feeling well today."

I feel a quiver of worry—is she avoiding me? I feel guilty all over again for my mean thoughts and feelings yesterday. "I hope she feels better."

"I'll tell her you said so." And Magnus pins me with a dark glance that tells me he knows all about the friction between us, and doesn't like it.

The next day's dance is the waltz, and my newest partner is a blond Adonis named David, a classically trained ballet dancer from a rich New York family that "would rather I did anything in life than dance ballet," he tells me, and our new choreographer, an Argentine ballroom coach named Pedro.

Even though waltz is one of my weakest steps, David and I move well together and our similar background training makes for a relatively mellow day of practice that flies by.

Throughout the day, I wonder what's going on with Pearl. Mom told me the whole family was leaving extra early for a day at Disneyland, and they'll just be making it back in time for the results show processing the voting from the night before, so there's no way to tell what's happening with them until after.

And Brandon? Well. After that scene in the elevator, it's better to just stay distracted.

The show is beginning to feel like it has a rhythm to it—an intense rhythm, but a real one. Every time I get a partner, I experience a new relationship with a guy. I've never been around so many this intimately before. My life until now basically consisted of school, home, and the Eureka dance studio. Now I feel like I'm on a fast-forward track, learning to deal with people.

Due to time constraints, I haven't gotten to know the other women on the show. They all paired up as roommates and know each other well by now. By rooming with Alex early on, I cut myself out of the female herd—and staying with him at the top of the hotel is a distinction not lost on anyone. I'm competition, not friendship material.

I don't think I'm imagining the cold shoulders and whispered comments I hear as I walk through the cafeteria and look for someone to sit with.

The only person sitting at a table alone today is Selina Sefton, the girl everyone's talking about as the best female dancer on the show. She's usually alone, and today she's seated at a round table in the corner, forking up salad.

I sit down with my tray. "Is this seat taken?"

"Does it look taken?" She has icy blue eyes and black hair and looks like she eats diamonds for breakfast.

I forge ahead with the niceties. "We haven't really met. I'm Jade."

"I know who you are."

This is not going well. I put my head down and scoop up my soup, chosen because it's low-calorie but makes me feel full. After the morning's workout with David, my stomach is rumbling.

She seems to relent. "I'm Selena. You and Ernesto were amazing last night."

"He's an exceptional dancer," I say carefully.

"He's exceptionally hot. Everything he does is hot. I can't wait to partner with him."

"He knows how hot he is," I warn Selina, meeting her gaze. I don't know how to say anything more about Ernesto, his confidence, his appeal, how he pushes things—and how he doesn't care who he hurts.

She seems to read my expression. "I'll be careful. I can take care of myself."

"That I believe." I address my soup. I'm surprised to hear Selina chuckle, and it's a small gurgling sound like a happy baby makes. "What's your dance background?" I ask her.

"I've been dancing ballet since I was three. I've had my eye on this contest since this show started, so I've been working with coaches for three years, hitting all the styles pretty thoroughly." Selina uses her knife and fork to cut her lettuce. "You?"

Selina's like an Olympic athlete that's trained her whole life and only had one goal: this show. I'm totally intimidated.

"Nothing like your background. I started dancing at fourteen, taking ballet at a storefront studio. I've pretty much lived there ever since, but only had a few ballroom lessons and I taught myself other styles by watching MTV music videos."

Selina's mouth hangs open, a forkful of lettuce halfway there. She puts her fork down and shakes her head. "That's amazing. Shows how talented you are."

I blush. "Just found something I love to do more than anything else."

"So are you and Alex—together?"

I remember that they partnered last night. "No. He's gay."

"I thought he was. But he sure knows how to turn on the x-factor dancing."

"You got that right. We met in San Francisco during the tryouts." We discuss the various competitors. It's a relief to have someone to talk it all over with.

Alex walks in with Ernesto. Ernesto's got his arm over Alex's shoulder in that sexy, "you're mine" way he has.

"Alex is mad at me right now," I tell Selina. "But I hope that's over." I gesture with my chin to the door.

"I get it." She's sharp, this girl. I scoot closer to Selina as Alex and Ernesto, carrying loaded trays, join us. I hate the way the guys eat like horses, and we have to count every fat gram.

"Yes! We get to sit with the two finest ladies on the show." Ernesto smiles with patented charm, but Alex still evades my gaze. I never saw him at all last night—his bedroom door stayed shut, and we missed each other in the morning.

"You two make up?" I ask.

Ernesto leans over and kisses Alex's cheek. "Getting there. He knows I just like to get into character."

"You're a character, all right," Alex mutters, sounding intentionally light. "Slut."

"Jealous bitch," Ernesto says calmly, picking up his burger.

"Whore."

"And you love me for it."

"Well. This has been great." Selina wipes her mouth on her napkin. "I've got to get back to it. I'm dancing with Hal this round —got any tips for me, Jade?"

I'm done with my soup, so I get up too.

"See you later, boys. Yeah, I have a few ideas." I follow Selina out, telling her about Hal's tendency to land heavy on his left foot and that he can get a little handsy. "What style are you two doing?"

"Contemporary. It's a really emotional piece, and he's pretty stiff, which is making me freeze up too. Really wish I had either of those two at the table for this number. Our choreographer is amazing, though—Rhiannon." I've seen the woman around—she wears nothing but black, and sports a huge, rainbow-colored Mohawk. I've been impressed by the contemporary dances that she's choreographed so far.

"I don't know what to tell you—slip Hal a Xanax?"

Selina laughs again, that baby burble. "I might have to try that! He leaves his water bottle lying around..."

I like her. It feels like a triumph. We talk and joke as we make our way to our practice rooms, and I hope that I might be making a friend.

Brandon

Another long day. I head for the monitoring booth to work the evening's results show, coffee and clipboard in hand.

I feel like I've been slogging through tar all day. Maybe it was the sleepless night last night, the room feeling way too empty— but when I looked through my address book of contacts for female company here in LA, none appealed. I just wanted to forget Jade and get laid, but it was all too much work.

I ended up going to the gym late and crashing in the sauna after my workout, hoping Jade would somehow show up.

Which, of course, she didn't. Girl had to get to bed early, as she'd clearly told me.

Not that I care, of course.

I'm pissed that I was disappointed last night, pissed that this sore tooth of a feeling is interfering with my concentration, and pissed because I should be happy right now.

The numbers came in today from the ratings company, and we're gaining viewers at an exponential rate every time the show airs. We've had moderate, steady growth each year, but this year looks like the one *Dance, Dance, Dance* officially becomes a hit. All of which looks good for another season next year. Now that I'm building my talent agency, another season is another opportunity for a rich fishing pool of possible clients, a likelier long-term success strategy than running a television show and hoping for a string of hits.

I've always known that directing a TV show wasn't my thing long-term, and after this season, with the crazy long hours and all the travel—I'm feeling a weird kind of exhaustion deep down.

I only forget it when I'm with Jade.

Screw that thought.

I reach the booth's door and push in. Tad from Yale jumps up out of my seat in the cockpit next to Brad the video editor. "Sorry, Boss. I was just getting a look at the dailies. Gonna have some interesting segments for tomorrow's competition."

"That better be the case." I slap down my coffee and clipboard on the desk. "Where's Clay? I want him down with the director tonight, helping him out and learning the ropes."

"Yes sir. I'll tell him. I have some items that need your attention, myself." Tad holds out his clipboard. "Had some deliveries that still need your signature, and here's a list of the injuries treated on the set."

I get that report every day and have to initial it as part of our insurance contract. I skim down and pause at Jade's name. *Minor head trauma and bruising to tailbone, hip and forehead*, reads the nurse's note.

My pulse speeds up. Will she be able to dance tonight?

Of course she will. Nothing short of a broken bone would stop her—and maybe not even that. Nor any of these competitors, come to think of it.

"Anyone have to call in the doctor today?" We keep a registered nurse who specializes in sports medicine on hand during the day, but we have a doc on call for more serious issues. Injuries are an inevitable part of a dancer's life, but I try to set up the show to do everything we can to minimize them.

"No doc calls. No hospital trips."

I initial the page. "From here on out, I want to be called anytime we have an injury bad enough to have the doctor called. Liability."

"You got it, Boss." Tad makes a note. Anytime I say "liability," people jump. I need to keep throwing that word around.

"Hey. Get me a beer, will you?" I hand Tad a five. "I know the caf doesn't have them, but the bar should."

"Sure, Boss."

"And thanks. Good job today." Tad looks downright perky after I compliment him. I wish it were that easy for me to feel better. At least I recognize that I need to take the edge off—hence, the beer.

Brad and I get started, talking on headsets with the director in the pit, Kate the emcee and the cameramen in their positions.

Jade and a new partner, that blond kid from New York, are working on a decent-looking but not particularly memorable waltz number in the practice dailies. I check for signs of her injuries, and can't see any evidence of them.

The girl might look and taste like a peach, but she's as tough as a tractor tire—something I need to remember.

Jade won't be in danger of getting booted off the show for a couple of days. Last night's piece with Ernesto was so strong that she should be okay for a while, and from what she told me, waltz and foxtrot are her two weakest steps and those will soon be out of the way. She still has ballet, contemporary and tango or cha-cha to go, and those she should do well at.

I shake my head and refocus on the screens in front of me. I'm over the whole thing. She's just another contestant.

The dancers file out after Kate does her witty/humble/touching intro and we have a solo performance from last year's winner...and no surprise, Jade and Ernesto are the highest-scoring performers from the night before. I'm becoming familiar with the sight of the Michaels family rejoicing in the audience.

I don't mind seeing them from a distance.

I stay in the booth until ten p.m., helping Brad and Alan sift through the footage from the day and begin the process of putting together the show. There's a lot more editing to do, but we get it roughed out at least.

I get up too fast and feel a wave of queasy dizziness. Stu, standing in the doorway, spots this of course. "Hey, man. When did you eat last?"

"Can't remember." I chuck the empty coffee cup and beer bottle into the trash. "I'll grab some room service."

"Nah. Come have a drink and a bite with me in the lounge. The appetizers there aren't too bad."

"All right." Stu's company is definitely preferable to the empty room and long night ahead.

We sit in one of the leather-padded booths and order a mess

of appetizers and a pitcher of beer. Life begins to look better halfway through the mountain of food.

"Thanks, Stu. I needed this."

"You looked like it." For a guy as skinny as a licorice whip, Stu can sure pack away the chow. He's on the second of three burgers. "What's eating you?"

"What do you mean?" I gesture to the spread. "I just got too distracted today. You know how I get. Tunnel vision."

"Nah." Stu takes a swig of beer, wipes his mouth, and sits back, "You're obsessing on that damn model and her family." Stu's known me since before that whole thing with Pearl got started four years ago.

"I'm not. I'm over it." I bite a chunk of chicken with my teeth and slide it off a kebab stick. "It's fine. Just pretty sure, even though the show's really taking off, that I need to find another main producer. Not doing this again next year."

"We've got the momentum now. You'll be able to afford someone good."

"Yeah. Because I'll be busy managing Forbes Talent—which will also own *Dance, Dance, Dance.* So things are on an upswing."

"I'll drink to your new empire." We bang beer steins.

"So why are you looking like road kill? I still think you need to get laid." Stu starts in on the platter of sushi.

"Not disagreeing with that. Just don't have time for all the games."

"I hear you. Which is why I'm glad to have an old lady to go home to." Stu's wife, Becky, whom he adores, is his physical opposite: a chubby, apple-cheeked woman with a ready laugh, Becky reminds me of a happy garden gnome. "You should think about settling down. It's not like women aren't throwing themselves at you."

"Don't have the time or energy for that shit." I finish my beer.

"Too much effort and drama. All that getting to know and pretending to care." I give a theatrical shudder. "No thanks."

"You just haven't met the right woman, and you're still just burned by Pearl dropping you. Don't forget, I knew you before, back when you were a romantic little rescuer." Stu wags his finger at me, referencing how I met Pearl in the first place—and discovered her for Melissa as a model. I was young, naïve, and hopeful back then—had a whole life for myself mapped out that didn't end up happening.

Stu and I met at MIT where I was majoring in engineering, that early attempt to break away from Mom. He was in a different program, but we hit it off over pool in the residence hall, and kept that bond through the changes in both of our lives since.

Stu goes on. "I get it. Pearl's one in a million. But so are you. Please. Do me and Becky a favor and go out with someone so we don't worry about you dying alone."

"Like Mom, you mean?" I don't know where that comment came from; it just popped out of my mouth.

"I didn't say that." Stu points his chopsticks at me. "You did."

Mom never recovered from Dad's death. Never even has dated anyone seriously since he passed. She's married to her work. Maybe that's changing, though, with this cancer scare. "I date. I go out."

"Yeah. You pick up women in bars and sleep with them once."

I gesture for the check but can't get the waitress's attention. "You know what? It's been a long day." I peel three twenties off and toss them onto the table. "Thanks for the nag session."

"Aw, hey, man," Stu says, but I just walk off, with a backwards wave to show him I'm not mad.

But he can't push me on this topic. It's off-limits—and so is my heart.

CHAPTER FIFTEEN

Jade

THE FAMILY MEETS ME IN the cafeteria for dinner, as we've been doing, but this time I invite Selina to join us. I introduce her, and the slight widening of her eyes is the only indication she gives that she knows who Pearl is. I'm relieved. Selina's so confident and self-contained that she doesn't need to gush over celebrities.

I'm also glad to see Pearl's back with us.

"Wow, Selina, you've really got moves," Ruby exclaims. "You're the only female dancer really giving Jade a run for her money."

Selina tosses her silky black hair. "Jade is a standout, that's for sure."

"I'm not feeling special in this next round." I sit between Ruby and Mom. "We did okay in practice today. Nothing to write home about. I hope it's enough to keep us on the show."

"You'll be fine." Selina, across from us and beside Pearl, flaps a hand. "You'll make it through the next few rounds because of the Ernesto glow."

"Yeah, that Ernesto is a crowd-pleaser. How was Disneyland today?" I don't want to hog the conversation. "Maybe, if you didn't hit all the rides, we could go again when the contest is over?"

"I'll go again!" Peter pipes up, and everyone laughs.

Selina and I hear about their adventures, and it's nice to get out of the closed-in world of dance and the contest for a few minutes.

Selina stands up with her tray. "Wonderful to meet all of you. Please pardon me, but I need to get to bed early tonight."

I start to get up too, but Ruby touches my arm. "Hey. I was hoping you, me, and Pearl could hang out for a bit. Sister time."

"Sure." I wave at Selina and sit back down, feeling a twinge of apprehension. Sister time isn't always good. Mom, the guys and Peter say their goodnights. Ruby takes care of the check. The cafeteria is bustling and noisy with post-show steam being blown off, and she clearly has an agenda.

"Let's go to the lounge, where it's quieter."

Pearl is withdrawn. She hasn't spoken more than a word or two through the whole evening. The two of us follow Ruby across the large, open lobby with its luxury furnishings to the lounge, dimly lit with a combination of low, backless benches set around tables for larger groups, and high, padded booths.

We take one of the booths. I slide in on one side, and Ruby and Pearl take the other side. I immediately feel ganged-up on, and hide it by picking up the menu. "I can't eat any of these desserts, but I'd love a drink if one of you could order for me."

"I need a drink too but I'm off booze—for the rest of my life. So what's this about, Ruby?" Pearl asks. Quiet and subdued is totally not her style. She's a fighter, and a mean one too, when she gets going. Her demeanor the last few days would have worried me if I weren't so busy being jealous of how she's still got Brandon wrapped around her little finger.

"I thought we should clear the air," Ruby says. "Talk about what's going on between you two."

The waitress arrives, and Ruby orders a Baileys Irish cream whiskey and a hot tea. Pearl orders a ginger ale, and I make do with water.

"I'm not sure how clearing the air is going to solve anything," Pearl says. "What we need is some hard core family therapy."

My mouth falls open in astonishment. "You're into therapy?"

"Yes." Pearl raises her eyebrows, widening her eyes sarcastically. "I've been clean and sober for close to five years—and I've gone to a lot of therapy since Dad died. But you probably tuned that out, like everything else I say or do." Yeah, Pearl can be a mean fighter, and she has a light in her eye like she's just getting started. Glasses of water arrive, and that gives me a tiny moment for rebuttal.

"Pardon me for not being in the worldwide Pearl fan club. I was too busy being the only kid at home with Mom and our grandparents while Mom tried to rebuild her life."

Pearl turns to Ruby. "See? We need family therapy." She turns back to me. "You didn't know what was going on with me back on St. Thomas, because you didn't want to know. I was date raped by the Carvers and intentionally hooked on heroin. Rafe and Ruby rescued me because Mom couldn't do anything with me. Maybe you remember that much—but all you did was wash your hands."

My hands, concealed in my lap, stop in mid-motion—I'm halfway through thirteen cleaning gestures with my hand sanitizer. I'm stunned by these revelations. I knew Pearl had boyfriends and was into drugs, but I had no idea it wasn't her own choice.

"No one here has the corner on pain and suffering," Ruby says quietly. "We've all been through a lot since Dad died."

"Says Miss-Super-Accomplished-Married-to-a-Millionaire." I

stop, then clap my hand over my mouth. "Ruby, I'm sorry. I don't know where that came from."

I adore my oldest sister and I know how hard she's worked at everything— including bringing and keeping our family together.

Ruby sighs. "Maybe that's how it looks on the outside. But I loved Dad so much. We were close in a way he wasn't with either of you, I hope I don't hurt you by saying that."

"We both know you were Daddy's girl," Pearl says. "It's okay." She takes a large swig of water and coughs.

"I don't see how this is accomplishing anything, and I need to get to bed," I say. "It's just upsetting me, and I need to stay focused."

"You've never had trouble with that," Pearl says. "What you've had trouble with is everything else. Everyone has to protect you, make things easier, because Jade is 'sensitive.'" Pearl made air quotes with her fingers. "Well, I can't help being who I am. I've tried to be a loving sister to you—but you won't listen to a thing I say or accept a thing I do to help. Even this." She gestures to the restaurant, encompassing the show and the situation with the tickets. "I called Brandon, my old boyfriend, and had a hella uncomfortable conversation because I was worried about you and wanted to make sure you were okay down here. And you do nothing but throw it back in my face."

The drinks mercifully arrive. Ruby fusses with her tea. Pearl and I gulp at our drinks. Even as upset as I am, the warm, sweet creaminess of the Baileys slipping down my throat tastes like ambrosia.

"I'm super grateful you got Brandon to give the family tickets, and you all came to LA to support me." I address Ruby. "What I'm not grateful for is that Brandon is still hung up on Pearl."

Both of my sisters widen their eyes.

"I thought I saw something might be going on between you

when he came into the caf that evening and you left together," Ruby says.

"Good going, Jade. He's a great guy," Pearl says. "There is nothing between us. Hasn't been for years." Her blue eyes, the exact same shade as Dad's, are sincere. "I love Magnus. He's the man for me. I'm seriously taken. Like, forever. Does Brandon need me to give him that message?"

"No." I look down at the snifter I'm holding with the delicious, calorie-laden swirl of creamy Bailey's in it. "Brandon knows that. But he's not over it. And I'm not willing to be your leftovers." I look up at Pearl as I sip deliberately. "I'm not ever being your leftovers again. In any way."

Pearl shakes her head. "That's all you, girl."

Ruby frowns. "I'm pretty shocked by that, Jade. None of us, Mom and Dad included, have ever thought of you as any kind of leftovers. We love you. We're proud of you. Maybe you're the one who has a chip on her shoulder and needs to prove something."

"Why do you think I'm in this freakin' contest?" I throw back the rest of my drink. It's a shame not to enjoy something that's costing me so many calories, but I can't stay here a minute longer. "I'll understand if you guys leave the show." I slide out of the booth.

"Running away is your style. Not ours," Pearl says. "We're not that selfish."

"Hey," Ruby moderates, but I'm done. I turn and leave.

On the elevator, I think of Brandon. Of last night's kiss. Of his face going cold. Of how I haven't seen him today, and how he walked away last night. Added to the talk with my sisters, it's all too much.

Crying feels like lancing the boil of pain tightening my chest —agonizing, and a relief—but the ache's still there, living in my bones.

Days go by in an ever-tightening spiral of stress as the contest moves forward relentlessly, demanding every ounce of effort and discipline I can give it. We continue to meet as a family in the cafeteria for dinners, and Ruby and Pearl keep things light and easy. By some miracle, I keep advancing in the show until I'm in the final four.

I don't see Brandon except at a distance: always wearing his headset, carrying his clipboard, in a hurry, never so much as glancing at me. I die a little bit inside every time I see him.

The final morning of the competition, wrung out from the emotional rollercoaster, I'm paired with Alex for a contemporary piece choreographed by Rhiannon for the final showdown. We're up against Ernesto and Selina, dancing tango.

The climax of the show being the four of us feels inevitable and fated—and scary as hell.

CHAPTER SIXTEEN

Jade

I'VE NEVER DANCED THIS HARD IN MY LIFE.

I seem to think that every day, but today it's really true. From the minute I found out that I'm dancing contemporary with Alex against Selina and Ernesto, I know I'll have to dig deeper, to a place I've never gone, to an emotional and physical level I'm not sure I'm capable of.

Working with Rhiannon is a whole new kind of heartfelt.

In the morning, when we meet her, she tells us about the "story" she wants us to show: one of intense first love, followed by betrayal, followed by reconciliation. She plays Bonnie Raitt's new song, *I Can't Make You Love Me*. The lyrics tell the story, the songstress's throbbing voice embodying the longing of haunting, possible love.

It chokes me up, just to listen to. I shut my eyes to keep the tears in.

Brandon has avoided me all week—the most I've seen of him was his back, at a distance. Whatever we had—those intense, stolen, magical moments, is over. Walking away from me and leaving me on the elevator was his answer to that hard question I asked about what I was to him.

I'm nothing to him.

It's easy to let the music bring my bruised emotions boiling to the surface—and glancing over at Alex, I see similar feelings brimming in his eyes.

Falling for a guy like Ernesto cannot be easy on the heart.

Rhiannon shows us some of her ideas for moves and turns off the lights.

She has us dance the emotions we're feeling in the dark, interacting closely with each other. At the end of our improv, I'm wrung out. Tears are drying on my cheeks. *Did I really just dance that?* Alex looks the same way—more than perspiring, it's like the sweat coming out of him is blood.

Rhiannon turns the lights on, hugs us, and kisses our foreheads. "Good. You're getting there. Let's map it out and nail it down."

We go through it again and again, and by the time it's time to dance the piece, I'm sure, in some deep place, that I'm living this song, this dance, because there's some greater force at work.

Maybe the God that I walked away from, the secure, familiar God I grew up with on St. Thomas—the God who abandoned us when Dad died—maybe He's not dead after all.

I was meant to go through this thing with Brandon, just so I could dance this piece tonight.

We're dancing this piece under a black light, with just a diffuse spot on us. Makeup and hair do their usual magic and put Alex and me in identical white leotards and tights, covered with lines of glowing paint picked out in dark jeweled rhinestones.

"You're an essence, not a character, for this dance," Rhiannon tells us. "Not just you, Jade, and you, Alex. You're everyone who's ever loved, lost, and reconnected. You're the spirits of that. So I want you to embody something better than human."

Something better than human.

I don't feel better than human. I don't feel like a spirit of anything but heartache.

Brandon

It's been unbelievably hard to stay away from Jade, to avoid even making eye contact with her, but I'm sticking to the resolve I made in the elevator.

I'm done— just wishing it wasn't so hard to move on. Juggling my briefcase and a Styrofoam cup of coffee as I cross the street to the studio in the early morning, I remember her face.

The way her waist felt with my hands spanning it.

Her delicious smell.

Her lips were so soft—and the way they opened under mine in eager surrender told me what the rest of it would be like, if we ever went to bed.

Something smacks me with the force of a giant's hand.

It hits me in the left hip, lifting me off my feet into the air so fast I can't even scream.

Hit by a car, my brain belatedly translates as I crash onto the hood of a taxi with a breath-stealing crunch. I roll off to land in the street, briefcase flying, coffee spraying everywhere in a hot gush.

I land face down on the asphalt and manage to break the fall with my hands and knees, but immediately hear a blare of horns and screech of brakes.

I'm not done getting hit.

The second blow is just a love tap: the kiss of a bumper hitting my raised shoulder and knocking me onto my face on the asphalt.

I lie there, face planted in the blacktop, stunned, as pinwheels and tweety birds circle my head. Yeah, they really kind of do that —though maybe they're more like stars.

But definitely, pinwheels are involved.

My lungs, forcefully emptied of air, struggle and finally kick in. I gasp and drag in gulps of air, opening my eyes.

I'm semi-beneath the second car. The bumper of the first car that hit me is about fifteen feet away, which tells me how far I flew.

"Oh my God! Are you okay?" A female voice drifts down from above. The voice sounds like it's calling from the top of a well. More running feet arrive. I hear them as vibrations through the road.

More hollow exclaiming voices.

I slowly lever myself up onto an elbow. "I'm okay."

And, astonishingly, I *am* okay. My cheek's smarting from gravel burn, my hip hurts like a mofo and my shoulder's wrenched, but I can already tell that nothing's broken. I drag myself to my knees in spite of the drivers' protests.

Onlookers fetch my briefcase and the empty coffee cup, offering both to me. That makes me crack up, and I laugh like a hyena.

The man driving the original car, a taxi, is Ethiopian: thin, tall, and so black his skin has a purple sheen. Distress makes him lose his English, and he exclaims in a language filled with liquid music. He grasps my arm, lifting it over his shoulder, and carries me to a nearby bench, where he pads my head on the Chicago Bulls sweatshirt he unzips and rolls up as a pillow.

An hour or two later, after being treated by ambulance personnel, tanked up on a fresh cup of coffee and a couple of Vicodin that the second driver slipped to me, I limp into the studio building carrying my briefcase.

Clay from UCLA meets me, cross-eyed with stress. "Where've you been, Boss?"

"Hit by a car." Moving is definitely an issue, I discover, as I head for the stairs up to the film editing office. "What's the current crisis?"

"Lot of phone calls about the final four. We've got a pile of agents wanting to sign them stuck in a waiting room and some calls from a music video company wanting to contract with us, and a lot of other stuff. Did you say you were hit by a car?"

"Yeah." There are five steps up into the video booth. I wonder if I can make them. "Gimme a hand here." One of Clay's shoulders beneath mine, I make it into the booth and ease into my chair next to Brad. "Get me a clean shirt and another cup of coffee, will you?" I brush at my coffee-stained shirtfront.

"Why don't I get the nurse?" Clay finally registers the road rash on my face and my generally wrecked appearance.

"Been checked out. Just some bumps and bruises. The show must go on." I've always wanted to say that, and this is my first time actually being able to. "Send my assistant Kerry in here. I want to talk with her about the agents and contracts for the final four."

Brad, beside me, has five o'clock shadow and it's only mid-morning. "Sure you should be here, Boss? And I'd rather you did that contract shit somewhere other than the video booth."

"It's getting to my office that's the problem. Get me that other intern—Tad. He can help me get up there." My lonely aerie of an office overlooking the big open practice area is a good destination to park for the day, but there are more stairs to navigate and no elevator. Once up there, though, there's a small seating area with a couch if I need to lie down, which I suspect will happen sooner than later.

Brad gets on the walkie and calls for Kerry and Tad from Yale to get me up to the office. "What's going on with the final four so far?" I focus with difficulty on the rack of screens before me.

"See for yourself." Brad points. "Selina and Ernesto are

heating it up in their tango practice. My money's on them to win." He taps their monitor. Even this early in the day, the pair generates crisp moves and palpable heat. "Jade and Alex are struggling a bit with Rhiannon, but that doesn't mean anything at this point—just means she's got a challenging piece for them, which could be good." He taps the monitor directly in front of me.

I squint and lean forward. That makes my cheek hurt, but the lighting is so dim I can hardly make out anything in the image. Rhiannon does things like that, turning off the lights in her studio and making her contestants practice in the dark, by feel alone, often without music.

I tap the audio feed, boost the sound. I can't hear anything but the shuffle of feet, the slide of flesh against flesh, the rasp of breath, and Rhiannon talking.

"I want you to feel this," Rhiannon says in the husky, hypnotic voice that I'm sure is a part of her success. "First, in your heart. The *love,* the passion! Then, the brokenness of betrayal, the agony of loss. The death of dreams. Once you can feel it in your heart, you can express it in your body."

"We can't pick up much footage to use in the teaser for tonight." Brad's loud, perky voice in the booth is a total mood killer.

"Rhiannon does this on purpose sometimes, when a piece is powerful. Means this one's gonna be good." I strain to see anything but two dark, moving shapes backlit by the red glow of the Emergency Exit sign. "We might not get any usable footage until one or two p.m., when she puts on the lights and music for final practice. But no worries. Cull the best bit of this, maybe that audio clip we just heard, and we'll do a pullout piece on Rhiannon and her choreography teaching methods."

Alex and Jade versus Selina and Ernesto.

The dancers' final pairings, and their showdown against each other, seem like they were meant to be. These four talented, charismatic dancers were always headed toward this moment—and the styles they're assigned are a perfect fit for their best skills.

Tonight will be a spectacular show.

Listening to the slide and slap of Jade's body against her partner's, her breathing as she dances an intense, emotional, physical piece in the dark, gets to me in a way I don't want to think about.

I'm over Jade.

I really am.

It's just my dick that still hasn't gotten the memo.

At least, that's what I tell myself. Loudly.

I cut the feed and move on to other screens.

"Oh my goodness, Brandon!" Kerry emotes as she arrives with Tad from Yale. "I heard you got hit by a car!"

"True. Help me get to my office. We have work to do."

I hope I can do something more than crash out on the couch.

Once physically relocated, Kerry helps me draft contracts to sign all four of the finalists to my newly formed Forbes Talent Agency. This completed step then enables her, with backup from my interns, to chase off the agents who've descended on the studio to try to snake my dancers.

I field phone calls and sign forms, and finally succumb to a lengthy nap on the couch.

"Did you get Jade to sign the contract?" I ask Kerry, when she finally wakes me up with a big glass of water and another pain pill. I stand up. I'm a little creaky but feeling a lot better.

Kerry shakes her head. "She wouldn't sign with your agency."

"What?" Surely the stab of paralyzing pain in my chest, right in the middle of my chest, is related to being hit by a car this morning.

"Jade said no, thank you. Said she had an offer from another agency and she was going to take it."

"Who?" Black spots are gathering in the edges of my vision.

"Jashon Mummings. He produces music videos."

I bite back a curse. Mummings is an unscrupulous dickweed whose videos are one step up from porn. Never mind that they sell well and get great ratings. Jade is all wrong for his venue.

I took too long to ask to ask her to sign with my agency, and now she's getting away. Once the show is over, she'll be gone. And I'm the one who walked away and left her in the elevator.

I sit down suddenly, because I have to.

CHAPTER SEVENTEEN

Brandon

A SHOWER FEELS GOOD ON MY battered body. Hands against the wall, water running down my hanging head and over my body, I think about life.

Getting hit by a frickin' car before your first cup of morning coffee will do that to a man.

Mom's got cancer. She has surgery scheduled, and as soon as she heals from that, begins chemo. I'm glad the show will be in the can by then, because I'll be flying back to Boston to be with her—and as hard as it is to face this when I've already lost Dad, the upside is that the crisis is bringing us closer.

I've called Mom every day since the diagnosis, and we talk more freely than we ever have—about everything. Not just the business.

I'm on track with my life in so many areas—the Forbes Talent Agency is getting off the ground with a bang, and Melissa's blessing. *Dance, Dance, Dance* is having its breakout season. I've got friends—I can't get rid of Stu even when I try. I have creative challenges that excite me, and whenever I miss engineering, I can just go backstage and work with the set designers and build something.

The thing I don't have figured out is love.

Am I going to die alone? It could have happened this morning. Am I so scared of being hurt that I won't take a chance again?

I don't know the answer. That feels shitty.

Jade's sweet face continues to haunt me.

Drying off, I take another pain pill and then dress in black slacks, a Gucci belt and loafers, a striped gray silk shirt. *When you're really hurting is the time to look your best.* Melissa taught me that.

I make my way down to the pit and sit with Alan, the director, right beneath the action. It's the last night of competition—all that's left will be filming the results show tomorrow.

And then she'll be gone.

"You look like shit," Alan spares a glance at my sorry ass.

"I thought I was hiding it."

"The clothes are all right. It's the shiner, the scrape, and the way you're moving like a ninety-year-old man that shows you were hit by a car today."

"Thanks for the compassion. Who's up first?"

"Ernesto and Selina."

The audience has filled in and the show gets underway. We go through the talky-talk from Kate, a performance by a group of Riverdancers, and then it's go time.

Ernesto and Selina blaze onto the stage and they literally look like they're going up in flames, dressed as they are in matching costumes made of red-and-gold glittering sequins held together with invisible netting and good intentions.

The chemistry between them makes every crisp, showy spin seem like foreplay; every kick, twist, and dip as they heat up the stage with their tango feels like the main event. Their moves are also technically perfect. These two embody everything tango is supposed to be.

Hope sinks for Jade and Alex.

Ernesto tosses Selina onto his shoulders for the finale, and she poses like a pinup girl, one leg hooked around his neck, the other pointed. She spreads her arms like Evita blessing her people as he slowly spins her.

The auditorium erupts in applause and a standing ovation.

"Damn," I mutter. "That was smoking hot."

"Yeah. Good luck to the other two. Cut to commercial," Alan says into his headset.

The curtains close. Props are moved and lights repositioned to prep for the next team while the crowd is entertained by Kate talking to the sparkling contestants.

"Smashing!" Kate says. "That was incredible. How did it feel to you?"

"Dancing with Ernesto is so amazing. We were born to tango." Selina's icy blue eyes flash and her blue-black hair shimmers under the lights, contrasting with her bright, glitzy costume.

"Yeah, and we do it so well, too." Ernesto grins naughtily, making the audience laugh. "Don't forget to call me." He recites his call-in voting number to the camera as if asking for a date.

Yeah, Selina's gorgeous and dances well—but it's Ernesto, with a long, muscular arm around her shoulder, that the cameras really love. The girls are going to fall all over themselves calling in to vote for him as soon as the show closes.

At least I got both of *them* to sign with Forbes Talent.

The buzzer sounds and the lights dim, signaling for the next contestants: Jade and Alex are up.

I straighten to watch from my vantage point roughly a foot or so above from the edge of the stage. This makes for a weird foreshortened view, but I can't stand to be away from where everything is happening, hiding behind a bank of monitors.

Not tonight. I want to be right in the thick of it tonight.

The curtains part. It's still dark onstage, but I can see Alex and Jade in their positions by an occasional gleam that gives them away. A black light spot comes up, and they're cast in an eerie, haunting glow like skeletons at a Grateful Dead concert.

Bonnie Raitt's new song, *I Can't Make You Love Me* wails out of the speakers, and the glowing dancers rise.

If Ernesto and Selina were all heat and technical perfection, Alex and Jade are all feeling. They begin with their arms hooked, back-to-back, and they roll end-over-end across the stage, playful, whirling. Then one breaks away, while the other becomes a hunched ball of weeping, kicked around by the other—and suddenly their positions reverse again.

The performance is mesmerizing. I clutch the edge of the stage, white-knuckled, as Jade, a whirl of glowing spangles marking her passage, somersaults past with Alex in pursuit. He captures her and lifts Jade high, all the way to the full of extent of his arms, holding her aloft by that tiny waist, his face a rictus of rage.

Jade's arms are spread, her toes pointed, her mouth a black hole of scream in her glowing face as he launches her, throwing her away.

The audience gasps, and the extreme move elicits cries from the crowd even as Jade lands in a roll that brings her bouncing to her feet, running back to 'kick' him into a back walkover—but then he stays down, on his knees. And, tentatively, he reaches out in entreaty with an extended hand.

She takes that hand.

They slide to the ground, their feet connected, and pull forward in foot-to-foot splits. There's a twisting, sensual recon-nection, embodying reconciliation, as Raitt's song throbs. They finish the piece standing as a perfect circle shape is created by their bent arms, legs and bodies.

I want to be half of that circle formed with Jade's body.

I'm not over her after all.

If I ever was.

Jade speaks through the dance, and the message seems meant for me. The delight of that first connection. The pain and hurt of rejection. The longing and hope for more. The rapture of reconciliation.

Alan breathes a curse. "Unreal."

The lights dim. The crowd goes nuts.

Jade raises her glowing face, breaking the circle shape, and looks right at me where I hover at the edge of the stage.

The curtain falls, breaking the spell between us. I am lost.

CHAPTER EIGHTEEN

Brandon

THE SHOW IS FINALLY OVER a couple of hours later, and I'm back at my room.

I'm pacing, even though walking still hurts my bruised body. I'm buzzing with tension, wanting Jade with a whole-body ache.

Yeah, the competition's basically over. Tomorrow's going to be editing and the results show—and then we're wrapped until next season.

Jade will be gone after tomorrow night.

Jade saw my face in the footlights as she danced, and she looked right at me at the end. I can still see her face, white and glowing, her eyes caves of mysterious darkness—but she broke the circle formed with Alex to turn her head and look right at me.

She knew where I was. She knew how closely I was watching.

I matter to her—whatever that look meant.

I've taken big risks before, on a lot less information than that. I'm done being a pussy. Trying to guard my heart. Truth is, I couldn't guard it from her even when I tried.

I yank the door open, resolved, and limp down the hall to the elevator. I stab the button—just as the doors open.

Jade's standing there in the elevator as if I conjured her with sheer wishful thinking. Her face is pink and fresh-scrubbed, her eyes very green. Her hair is dark and wet, streaming over the shoulders of a white hotel bathrobe that engulfs her from throat to knees.

I've never seen anything sexier in my life.

The door starts to shut and we both reach out to stop it at the same time, our hands colliding. I grab onto hers as the doors open again, and draw her toward me. "I was coming to see you."

"You were? Because I came to see you."

We stand awkwardly, facing each other, just outside the elevator's closed doors. Could she be naked under that robe? A throb from my groin casts a hopeful vote. *I'm such a classy guy.*

"We should talk." I reach out and take one of her hands, slowly, hoping she won't bolt. "Can we go to my room for some privacy?"

"Better than here in the hallway." Her hand is small, but I can feel how strong she is when she squeezes mine.

"All right then." My tongue feels too thick in my mouth. I can't think of how to proceed, what to say, as we head back to my room. I key open the door and hold it ajar for her. "After you."

She walks in ahead of me. Her mahogany-red hair catches a gleam of light from the uncovered window facing the sparkling lights of the city. From behind, her feet bare, she looks about twelve.

I feel a quiver of doubt. She's too young. Pearl's little sister. I can't hurt her.

Jade drops the robe. My breath seizes up. She's naked, and she doesn't look twelve any longer.

Long legs, perfectly shaped, are topped by a round, high, heart-shaped butt that flows into that tiny waist and then back out again to strong shoulders. I take a step toward her, swallowing, as I notice every detail: pale silky skin covering the bumps of her spine. Thumbprint dimples at her hips. The triangle of her shoulder blade.

"You're so beautiful." I'm so close to her now that the silk of my shirt brushes her skin. I don't remember moving, but there I am, my mouth next to her ear, my voice raising the hairs on her arms.

She turns, and tips her face up to mine. "I had to try one last time. To be with you."

I can't believe she's here, that she wants this as much as I do. I wrap her in my arms and lower my mouth to hers, telling her with my kiss how much I want her.

Jade whimpers, twining herself around me like a vine around a tree, and all is a bit of chaos for a while until I'm aware of her plucking and tugging at my clothing, and I hear "not fair, I want you naked too," in the murmurs coming from her plump, sweet, tasty mouth.

"I must be dreaming." I tug her by the hand and head for the bedroom, tearing at my buttons one-handed. "Am I dreaming?"

Jade sits on the bed. In front of me. I remember her in that position in the sauna: her little, round, creamy breasts with their tender nipples, the vanilla of her skin, the plume of dark hair at the apex of her thighs, the sheen of her hair.

"Let me." She pulls my shirt out of my pants and begins unbuttoning as my hands caress her wet hair, her shoulders. My fingers stroke and caress one perfect breast—it's as exquisite as summer fruit in my hand.

Parting my shirt, she gives a cry. "Brandon! Who hurt you?"

"A taxi." I look down the expanse of my bruised body. "Got hit by a car going into the studio this morning. Gave me a pause to think about priorities."

"Oh, my God." Her fingers gently slide over my bruises as she takes inventory, making me shiver, the hair rising on my body along with my erection. I'm harder than ever, a pulsing thickness straining the zipper of the tailored pants.

"I'm fine. That'll teach me not to look left when crossing the road."

"You could have been killed." Jade finds my waistband as my hands fist in her hair. Her voice thickens. "I might never have seen you again."

I can't think with her mouth that close to my erection.

"I'm fine," I repeat. "But I need to be in you. Soon. Or I'm not going to be fine."

She laughs, a sound that makes me weak in the knees, and tugs down the zipper. She pulls off my pants and boxers and I groan at the sensation as she touches me, still light, still tentative, but increasingly confident. She uses her fingers, her mouth.

"Like this?" she asks. "Or like this?"

"Just. Don't. Stop," I beg, and she laughs again, this time a throaty chuckle.

But, eventually I do have to stop her, because I don't want it to be over too soon. "Please. Let me. It's your turn."

Jade ducks her head, and that long hair hides her face. "I'm feeling shy. I can't believe we did that—you know. Before. That thing. I've been thinking about it ever since."

That makes the blood surge through me, throbbing painfully. "Me too. And there's another thing we're going to do, if you're ready. But I want you to be really ready. Because they say that sometimes your first time can be painful."

I'm thankful she doesn't argue. Instead she nods, still hiding.

I have to woo her out from behind her hair, but I'm impatient now—because that nod was a yes and I'm hungry for her: for all the ways I can taste, and feel, and take her.

I push her back on the bed, grasp her by the hips. "You're going to like this."

Jade

I think I'm going to die any second now. Surely that's where this is headed. Death is at the end of this galloping train of thundering heart, wound-up tightness, this sense of a golden ring just ahead if I can only reach it... I can't stop tossing my head, and the sounds coming from my throat are someone else, surely, wanton as they are, mainly consisting of his name and *please, please, please, oh yes.*

I'm ascending to a crest, my hands in his hair, and everything in me has become focused on this one, white-hot spot that contracts, drawing breathlessly tight, every muscle locked and rigid, sucked into a black hole of feeling; then, BOOM, it expands, rippling outward across my body, waves and waves of ecstasy that I can do nothing but ride... Until they wash me up on the beach of *after*, boneless as a jellyfish.

"Mmm, that was good." Brandon kisses his way up my body as I slowly return to it.

He was impatient before, and he still is. I feel it in the tension of his shoulders beneath my hands, in the slight tremble of his lips as they touch my breast, nip along my collarbone, as they find that tiny nook behind my ear and make me sigh.

"Are you ready for me?" Brandon asks, and I feel the length of him against me, hot and heavy.

"Yes," I breathe against his lips. "Oh yes."

He raises his head. "Damn. A condom. I must have one somewhere."

"In the pocket of my robe." I cast my eyes down modestly.

Brandon rears up and laughs. "You have a condom in the pocket of your robe?"

"Alex had some lying around. It seemed like one might come in handy."

He surges up off the bed, and I love to watch him move: the lamplight falling on his long back, gilding the golden hairs of his body, sliding over the solid lines of his legs and the tight rounds of his buttocks. The bruises marring his skin make him even more beautiful to me—he was almost killed this morning.

Walking back toward me, he's even better to look at: the broad square lines of his shoulders, the planes of his pecs, the ridges of his abs—and his male hardness leads the way.

"I'm not sure things are—going to fit." My voice has gone squeaky. "Pretty sure that's anatomically impossible."

He chuckles, a sound I feel as a vibration as he lies down beside me, stroking me from hip to breast and back again, every touch leaving my skin yearning for more. "And I'm pretty sure both of us have a secret expansion pack just for times like these. We'll take it slow."

He keeps up the stroking, and leans over to suck my nipple, drawing my breast deep into his mouth, then flicking me with his tongue. Within seconds, I've forgotten the intimidating sight of him walking toward me and feel that yearning again, that pushing, that craving for something nearby, promising amazement.

I reach down between us and my hand encircles his shaft. I like how it feels, like silk over steel, as I explore it. He hisses through his teeth. "Don't. Move."

"Perhaps it's time for the jacket." I pluck the condom off the comforter beside him and rip it open with my teeth. "I saw this in health class in seventh grade. With a banana. I think I can do it."

He makes a strangled groan of a laugh as I fit it on and roll it down, and then he immediately surges up over me, arms bracing his body above me, his thigh parting mine. "I know I said we'd take it slow—but I want you so much." Sweat shines over his shoulders, his forehead gleams, and his hazel eyes are intent on mine. "Do you trust me?"

"I do." The words sound like making a vow.

He's at my entrance, and it feels tight, and full, but good. So, so good.

Encouraged, I pull him closer and wriggle my hips to get him deeper.

With a muffled curse, Brandon sinks into me all the way—past a minuscule resistance that, for a dancer, barely registers as a twinge of pain. Sunk deep in me, holding himself up on bunched, tight arms, Brandon's voice is taut. "You okay?"

I stroke my hands up his arms, touched by his concern, but as impatient as he is.

"Yes!" I tighten my abs and sit up partway to slide my hands around and grasp him by those hard buttocks, pulling him in. "Yes!" I've had enough slowness and holding back.

He surges deep with a heart-groan, then back, then forward again. I arch beneath him, feeling strangeness, fullness, the friction of tissues unused to such activity—but no real pain. And soon, a very real building, a pressure of need. "Yes, yes, more, yes!"

And he does give me more, a most glorious pounding *more*... and it tips us both over the edge of frantic striving into bliss.

CHAPTER NINETEEN

Brandon

I DON'T WANT TO LEAVE HER. I stay inside, propped on my elbows, looking down into Jade's face, smoothing her hair back gently.

"I'm sorry I was such a jerk. Walking away from you on the elevator like that. I've missed you every day since."

"I'm sorry that happened too." Her eyes flutter shut. *She's thinking of Pearl.* I feel the ghost of that conversation rising up, the bold question she asked—what is she to me? It's a chill wraith ready to steal the bond between us.

"Forget all that. We're here now. Together."

"Yes, we are." She lifts her head and kisses the hollow of my throat.

"Are you sure you're okay?"

"I am. Ruby told me her first time was awful—but that was no more than a pinch. Maybe all the dancing—I don't know. Took care of it somehow." Jade's still not looking at me and her cheeks are pink as she turns her face away. "Let's get a shower. Let me up."

She's trying to withdraw from me, and I don't like it. But crowding her might make it worse.

"If I must." I roll to the side and we head to the bathroom together. I flush the condom and follow her into the glassed-in shower cubicle "I was thinking of you before the performance. Right here in this shower. I can't believe that, just hours later, you're here with me."

"Yeah. I was thinking of you too. All through the performance."

She's saying the right words, but she's still got her back to me. Won't meet my eyes. She has the flowery-smelling bar of hotel soap in her hands and she's rubbing it with quick precise motions, and I see her lips moving.

She's counting.

"Do you have OCD?" The recognition of her symptoms pops out of my mouth just as it hits my brain, and I desperately wish I could take the words back as she freezes. I bracket her in against the wall of the shower with my arms. "Because I don't give a shit if you do. It would just help me understand what you need, how to help—if I knew."

Jade leans her forehead on the cool tile, her eyes closed. "Yes. I'm so embarrassed."

"Don't be. We all have things we struggle with." I press up against her from behind. "Want to get clean? Let me." I pluck the soap from her hands, soap my own hands until they're foamy, and set the bar in the holder. I spread my fingers and slide them up and down her back, shoulders, arms, into the deep and secret places of her body, the tender areas. Her breath comes faster and faster as she presses against the tile, her eyes closed, her hair a long dark river pooling water in the hollow of her lower back.

I trace the pearl-like string of her spine, sliding down between her firm buttocks and between her legs, reaching around beneath her to cup her. One finger slides into her, finding that tiny gem that I seek. She rears back, slamming into my body with a gasp of aroused surprise, and that lets me sink my fingers deeper into her.

I love the feeling of her butt against my forearm. *Ah yes.* She wants me again, and it's a good thing because I want her again too.

"Oh! Oh!" she cries, as I keep working her.

I latch onto her neck with my lips and teeth. It sends her over the edge as I give her a hickey right on the same spot where she gave one to me so many days ago.

"Mine," I growl, through the welter of her climax against my hand. She seems about to collapse as the sensual pulses fade, sliding down the wall of the shower, so I turn her to face me. "My turn."

The smile Jade gives is incredibly beautiful. Her lips are red, her eyes the hazy green of a cedar grove in deep shadow. "Yes, it is."

I heft her up, lifting and sliding into her at the same time, settling her legs around my waist. All is wet, warm, slippery goodness, the shower filled with our sounds of pleasure as she slides up and down the wall, clutching my shoulders, my hair. My hands are filled with her, my mind is empty of anything but this moment, and like salmon leaping in a stream, we're driven toward a glorious end.

Thankfully my brain sends a last warning shot across the bow before disaster strikes, because I barely remember that I can't come in her—that I don't have a condom on. I get out in time, convulsing against her side, and she whimpers in disappointment. She slides her hands around to stoke my waist, hips, lower back.

"You have to get on birth control," I mutter into her neck. "I'm clean, and I kind of hate condoms, but we can't take this kind of chance again."

"Okay," she says. I hug her close.

She said okay.

'Okay' implies a future. And lots of sex without a condom.

I don't remember ever feeling so happy or so good.

Jade

We're still in the shower, plastered together in the longest, sweetest hug—but we're getting pruney now.

"Do you feel clean enough?" Brandon asks into my ear as he tenderly nibbles it.

"Any cleaner, and my skin's going to peel right off."

"Are you sure? Is there a magic number of times I should be doing something to make it feel right?" He's still nibbling and kissing, and shivers of pleasure chase each other over my skin.

"Thirteen," I whisper. "Thirteen is my magic number."

"Okay. We're going to stay in here and do it thirteen times."

My eyes pop open and I push him away, only to see his laughing face looking down at me. I can't help smiling back. "I never joke about—this."

My OCD. My shameful weirdness.

"It's time to start." Brandon's still smiling. Not mocking or mean. Just teasing in a loving way. "Like, can I give you thirteen kisses right here?" He leans down to kiss the top of my nose. "Will that make it better?"

"It's a start." I shut my eyes. He kisses my nose thirteen times. It makes me laugh, but it also feels exactly right—the way I need things to feel sometimes, when the world is changing too fast for me.

"There. Now we can get out." Brandon snaps off the water and opens the shower door. He pulls a big, fluffy bath towel down from a shelf and wraps me in it before getting his own. "Are you hungry?"

"As a matter of fact, I am. I ate before the performance, but..."

"I'd say you burned a few calories doing that piece. Incredible, by the way. I thought no one could beat Ernesto and Selina after their tango, but you two—so much heart. You have a real chance to win tomorrow night." His words warm me somewhere deep. Somewhere that longs for that kind of validation—and he's the producer of the show. He would know. Brandon shrugs into his hotel robe, and heads for the phone. "You can afford a few calories tonight—besides, you're going to need them later." He wiggles his brows at me and calls room service.

I walk across the silky plush carpet and pick my robe up from the floor where I let it drop. I still can't believe I had the courage for that bold move. I surprised myself. But after the show, after I cleaned off that glowing body paint, I just had to see him.

In my bathrobe. With a condom in my pocket, and my heart in my eyes. Thank God it worked, or I'd be doing something nuts right now like counting all the tiles in the bathroom while lying on the floor in the fetal position.

And he was coming to see me, too. The elevator door opened, and Brandon was standing there, so handsome, so perfectly dressed. His eyes lit up and a smile split his face, like me in my bathrobe was everything he'd ever hoped for.

I couldn't handle it. I had to look at the floor.

Sometimes, I know I won't be able to handle it. Any of this, even the amazing moments—but I'll just have to keep trying.

Brandon hangs up the phone. "I think we should find something fun to do while we wait for the food. I was thinking you might need a massage after all that dancing."

"Really? I *am* kind of sore."

He grabs me up and carries me to the bed. "I think you might enjoy this. Again."

CHAPTER TWENTY

Brandon

We don't sleep much that night and that's the way we both want it. What is happening between us eclipses any other relationship I've ever had like a supernova. Turns out I never had any idea about any of it.

I can't get enough of her: her firm tight body, her silky secret places, the way she moves like poetry. Even her insecurity fascinates me, the way she shies away if I look at her too long, the way she lies on her back and counts the pattern on the ceiling, her lips moving in her silent mantra of thirteen—ah, *thirteen*. Thirteen is my new favorite number.

I cut thirteen pieces of juicy room service steak for her. I pour thirteen splashes of wine into her glass. I rub her body with thirteen pumps of flower-scented hotel lotion.

Jade loves it, but by the morning she's laughing, begging me to stop with the thirteen business, she's over it already.

I hope that's true, but even if it isn't, I don't care. She's all I want, so damn perfect. Thirteen thousand times better than any woman I've ever been with.

She's finally sleeping when I wake at six a.m. per usual. I call down to her room, and Alex answers the phone.

"Jade's with me," I say without preamble when he answers. "I need you to bring some of her clothes to my room."

Alex chortles. "I told her last night—'you go, girl.'"

"Well, if you encouraged her to make a move—thanks. I was on my way to see her too, so it worked out." I rub the back of my neck and clear my throat. "So, can you please bring her something to wear? I have to get to work and I don't want Jade wandering the hotel in her bathrobe."

It makes me feel good to think of ways to make her happy, to make things a little easier for her. I'm bummed that I have to work on the show while she and the other dancers get their first real day of rest before the filming of tonight's results show.

Not that we'd get any respite if I were in the room with her all day...

I dress quickly and write Jade a note, and I'm just in time to bring in the flowers I ordered and set them up with the note, and an extra key to the room, beside the bed.

Now I'm off to deal with the wrap-up show. Today's prep is extra involved—it's the climax of the whole season, and the show's going to be an extravaganza.

Extravaganzas don't happen on their own.

I'm getting ready to cross the road to the studio, coffee in hand, looking both ways this time—when I remember I never talked to Jade about that sleazy video producer, Jashon Mummings.

That's okay. We'll have plenty of time to hash over what the next steps are for her career after tonight—because, whether she wins or not, it's taking off.

Jade

I wake up to a far-off muffled pounding and the sound of my name being called. "Jade!"

Alarm jangles through me. I sit up and toss back the covers.

I'm stark naked.

In Brandon's bed.

My cheeks get hot as I remember last night. Yeah, that tops the chart of my current life experiences.

The pounding starts again. Someone's at the door.

I glance over at the bedside table, and my heart jumps. A giant bouquet of peach-colored roses, laced with baby's breath and fern, is set beside a folded piece of paper. A room key weighs the note down.

Brandon had to go to work today. He told me last night he was going to be eyeball-deep in the show.

But he left me flowers. And a note. And a key.

I don't have time to investigate though. I have to find my robe and answer the door.

My body is pleasantly achy and there's an unfamiliar throb between my legs as I get out of bed, pick up my fallen robe, and put it on. Just walking across the expanse of creamy shag sets up tingles and twinges from various places unused to all the activities we got up to last night—but I'm certainly not complaining.

I peek through the lens just as the pounding begins again. It's Alex, holding something in his arms. I open the door. "Hey."

Alex rakes me with a glance. "You look—debauched."

I laugh. "I am. Come on in."

"Brandon called early this morning to ask me to bring you some clothes." Alex pushes a pile of garments into my arms. "Here."

"That was incredibly thoughtful of him." I hug the clothes against me. I can't stop smiling.

Alex looks around. "This is pretty much the same as our suite."

"Yeah." I go back to the bedroom and retrieve the note, key, and flowers.

"Sweet baby." Alex puts his hands on his hips, grinning. "Now that's a bouquet."

"He left a note, too." I open the folded paper. His hand-writing is bold and slanting, a mix of block letters and cursive as unique as he is.

Dear Jade,

It's actually physically painful to leave you right now, and if it weren't for the show I'd spend the day with you in bed... but alas. I wanted to tell you in writing how amazing you are, how incredible it was to be with you last night. I will miss you every minute until I see you again. Peach reminds me of you—and don't forget to count the roses.

~Love, Brandon.

The huge, orangey-pink buds are just beginning to open. I count the blooms, and my eyes fill with tears. I cover my mouth with a hand.

"What?" Alex asks.

"Thirteen. There are thirteen roses here." I burst into tears. "I can't believe this is happening to me."

Alex hugs me, strong and reassuring, smelling of lemony aftershave. "Whatever he did, I'll try to kick his ass for you."

"No! It's just that—this is all too good to be true. I'm the unlucky sister, always have been, and now..." I can't put into words how overwhelmed I am by incredible feelings, by what's happened on the show, by how my tiny little life is expanding. "I don't know how I can handle all of this—and I think I'm in love with him."

"Well, duh. And it seems to be mutual." Alex plucks the note from my fingers. "Mind if I read?"

I shake my head and he scans the note. "He doesn't say 'I love you,' but he pretty much does. And whether or not we win, with him in your corner, your career is going to take off. Did you sign with his agency yesterday when the girl with the contracts came around?"

"No. I wasn't sure I wanted to keep having to deal with how painful it was to be around him." I hang my head. "Did you talk to that video producer, Jashon Mummings, too?"

A big black guy in a pinstripe suit with a shiny bald head approached me as I was leaving the cafeteria yesterday. He complimented my dancing and told me he had a contract ready for me. I'd left with his card in my hand, and an appointment to meet with him after the results show.

"No. But why wouldn't you want to sign with Forbes, regardless? Brandon and Melissa are the names to be associated with in this town." Alex is frowning. "I bet that stung when Brandon heard you turned his contract down."

"Well, I was just—that was before." I snatch the note back. "We'll work it out. I didn't meet with Mummings yet."

"Fine. Well, today's our day off. What do you want to do?"

"Go to Disneyland." My face breaks into a smile as I run back into the bedroom. "Let me get changed, then I'll see what the family is up to."

Ruby, Rafe, Peter, Alex and I spend a blissful day at Disneyland as Pearl, Mom and Magnus opt for a quiet day in Los Angeles doing art museums. Shrieking through the dark on the newly opened Space Mountain rollercoaster, holding my nephew Peter's hand, I decide that the only thing better than this moment would be to have Brandon with me, too.

A sense of unreality, of being in a bubble of happiness too good to be true, persists through the day.

Back at the hotel, I say goodbye to the family until after the show, feeling worry niggle at me that I haven't resolved things with Pearl since that ill-fated evening with Ruby. And I still need to straighten out that contract thing with Brandon.

I'll take care of all of that after the show. After we find out who won.

It feels weird to get all painted up in our glowing paint and sequins and not dance, and glancing over at Alex, I can see he's feeling the same thing.

Walking behind Ernesto and Selina toward the main stage, I lean over to my partner. "Are you okay? With Ernesto?"

He shrugs. "Not everybody gets a happy ending. He's banging anyone that will hop in the sack with him, and I'm just not okay with that."

I put my hand in his and squeeze as we follow the other couple.

We wait backstage and finally they signal Ernesto and Selina to go out in front. The crowd goes wild, the show plays highlights from each of their dancing, and finally they take their seats in the empty bleachers that held twenty contestants when we started.

It's our turn.

The lights are blinding, the applause overwhelming. My hands are instantly sweaty and I let go of Alex's hand, needing to use my sanitizer and unable to, paralyzed with stage fright for the first time on the show.

Alex grabs me and raises both of our hands above our heads.

The clapping sounds like a thunderstorm breaking over a

rainforest, but the spell is broken and I can smile. We head to the bleachers as they play clips of us on the show.

Once seated, the spotlights off us, I scan everywhere for Brandon. High above, in the glassed-in observation booth in the center of the ceiling, I spot a white piece of paper with a heart drawn on it in Sharpie.

That heart is for me. He's up there in the booth.

I let my breath out with a whoosh and wave at him.

The lights go down, and a troupe of Russian ballet dancers takes the stage as the director prolongs the agony of the winners' reveal for maximum effect. A couple more performances, including the "All-Stars" of the last seasons' shows doing a mixed piece, and then it's the moment of truth.

The lights come up. Kate, wearing a tiny red dress, invites the four of us down to the front.

I can hear my blood roaring in my ears, and I clutch the lifeline of Alex's hand on one side, and Selina's on the other. I'm aware, so aware, of Brandon up in the booth, watching.

I wish it were his hand I'm holding.

Whatever happens, I'll be with him again tonight. *Everything will be okay once I'm in his arms.*

"It's time," Kate says. She holds the large white envelope with its gold seal aloft. The sound of the seal breaking sounds like a pistol shot in the waiting silence.

"And the winners are... *Selina and Ernesto!*"

The roar of the crowd is surf in the background. I'm frozen as a pillar of salt, unable to move or breathe. Balloons and confetti rain down on us. Ernest and Selina swirl through the falling debris in an impromptu tango, kicking balloons out of the way.

Alex is still holding my hand. He gives it a tug, pulling me into his arms. I'm jerky as a marionette as he moves me around the stage.

Alex murmurs in my ear. "Doesn't matter. *Doesn't matter.*

We're still winners. The world is our oyster, girl, we're winners. What a way to kick off our dance careers, we're the top two contestants after them..."

My good luck was too good to be true.

Ernesto and Selina, radiant and glittering, embrace us. Making the best of it, happy for them, we all dance around as a foursome. But I start counting my steps. "One, two three, four..."

I'm numb and distant from my feet.

Things to count are all around me. Balloons. Spirals of confetti. Stage lights. The steps of our dance. My family, ascending the stage, along with Alex's, Ernesto's and Selina's, just interrupts the flow of soothing numbers.

CHAPTER TWENTY-ONE

Brandon

JADE LOOKS LIKE A POSSUM just before road kill as the results announcement is read. My stomach churns at the sight of her stricken, pale face.

Thank God for Alex, taking her in his arms, talking to her, getting her moving... I can't wait to hold her, soothe her, take her mind off the loss as I tell her the truth—the big money is in the contracts that follow the show, not the contest purse or the temporary glow of the stage lights.

I'll have to tell her that in person, which won't be for an hour at least, as we wrap the filming and deal with all the myriad details of putting a major production show to bed at last.

But finally I can tear myself away, handing off my clipboard and producer chair to Clay. I check around the backstage area, hoping she's there, but the place is empty as a plague ship. I peek into the cafeteria and spot her family, but she's not with them. Maybe Jade's already back at my room, waiting for me.

I'm glad I left her the extra key by the flower arrangement. My heart speeds up in anticipation of seeing her. All day I've been thinking about her: flashbacks of her scent, the feel of her hands on me, the heft of her in my arms.

No one's in my room, but the note and flowers are gone. I hop in the shower to clean the sweat of the day off and wrap up in a towel.

There's a rap at the door. I'll have to remind Jade that she has a key. I pull open the door.

"Pearl," I say dumbly, looking at her sister. "What're you doing here?"

Pearl looks pale, but there's a determined set to that mouth I'm so familiar with—that mouth they share. She keeps her eyes on mine, not so much as glancing at the whole lot of nothing I'm wearing but a towel. "Can I speak to you a moment?"

"Sure." I hold the door open and she enters. The door drifts shut behind us. "What's going on? Is something wrong?"

"You could say that." The seventh most beautiful woman in the world is wearing a form-fitting black tunic top over leggings and boots, with a fat pearl on a long snake chain that dangles between her breasts. I remember when she got that gift for her nineteenth birthday. "Why haven't you signed Jade with Forbes Talent?"

"My assistant took the contract around to Jade yesterday and she refused to sign it." I run a hand through my wet hair. "I was planning to talk to her personally about it now that the show's over."

"Well, please move fast. I saw that sleazy porn video producer talking to her in the hall. I'm worried about him getting his hooks into her. Jade still thinks..." For the first time, a little color comes back into Pearl's cheeks. "Jade still thinks there's something going on between us, and she won't listen to anything I say."

"What? Between you and me?" I can't even calculate this, it's so over. "Oh no. Not after last night, she doesn't think that."

"What do you mean?"

I start to answer, but we both turn our heads at the sound of a key in the door. It opens, a slow-motion train wreck that I can't seem to stop.

"Pearl?" Jade's scrubbed clean, all the performance paint gone, but she goes white as she stares at us, green eyes wide. "I guess I interrupted something."

I glance down at my towel and bare feet. The bottom of my stomach does an elevator drop.

"No, no, I was just here for a second and now I'm leaving." Pearl's hands lift in a 'surrender' gesture.

Jade pulls the room's door shut.

I lunge forward and yank it open, darting after her. "Jade!" She's sprinting and somehow reached the elevators already. "Jade! No! It's not what you think!"

She looks at me wildly, stabbing the elevator button. I'll never forget the devastation in her eyes as long as I live. I run down the hall toward her, but she's faster, hitting the stairwell and disappearing.

I clutch my towel with both hands and curse like a truck driver.

Jade

I knew it.

Nothing ever works out for me, and no matter how many ways I invoke thirteen, I'm cursed. Clattering down the stairs at top speed, I still manage to count, getting to thirteen and starting over again.

Thirteen. My lucky number.

Thirteen bites of steak. Thirteen splashes of wine. Thirteen pumps of lotion. Thirteen kisses on my nose. Thirteen peach-colored roses.

Thirteen ways to blow it all to hell.

It's imperative that I get far away from Brandon, and that he not catch up with me. I can't handle it. I just can't handle it.

Brandon, wearing nothing but a towel and wet hair. Brandon, with his gorgeous, ripped body still sporting bruises, alone with my sister, his first love, in the hotel room where he took my virginity.

The pain feels like I'm being murdered—stabbed maybe, or strangled—but somehow I'm still breathing and moving.

I end my headlong flight when there are no more stairs to go down.

I'm in the hotel basement, in the laundry room. Giant machines whir and gurgle. Startled-looking employees turn to stare as I run, dodging around obstacles, through the room, seeking an exit. I know I'm acting like a looney tune but am unable to process how to get out—until finally, one old woman lifts a gnarled finger to point at a lit red Exit sign.

I hit the door bar and the steel door dumps me into a cement well in an alley at the back side of the hotel. A short flight of stairs leads up to the street. The alley is dark, lit by yellow pools of light, and the air smells like the dumpsters clustered around a service entrance.

I slow to a walk and head for the brightly lit street. I'm wearing a pair of athletic shoes, jeans, and the *Dance, Dance, Dance* T-shirt that Patty gave me in a swag bag from sponsors. Perhaps it's the shirt, a neon aqua and purple with gold lettering, that catches the eye of a reporter, talking to a cameraman next to a TV van parked at the corner.

The tailored-looking brunette swivels on an alligator heel and hobbles toward me as fast as her pencil skirt will allow, holding out a mic, the cameraman trailing in pursuit. "Jade! Jade Michaels! Give us a statement!"

Just like earlier in the evening, I freeze as the camera finds my face, lighting me up, stopping me in my tracks like a criminal caught in a jailbreak. The team zeroes in on me.

"Hi, Jade. Thanks so much for speaking with us. I'm Rosa Pinkins from WRBX LA. What's it like to come in second place on the hottest show in Hollywood?"

I muster a smile. "Oh, I can't believe I made it that far, truthfully. It was a dream come true to compete on the show."

"But you must have been disappointed when the results came in." Rosa Pinkins has a feral gleam in her eye. She's a cougar about to land on my back and break it with one snap of her veneered teeth. "I'm sure you wanted to come in first."

"Sure, that would have been nice—but Alex and I both have bright futures ahead in dance. I'm accepting a contract with Mummings Video Productions, and Alex is signing with the Forbes Talent Agency. You'll be seeing a lot of us in upcoming music videos, commercials, and anywhere a good dancer is needed." I smile as big as I can. "I'm just so glad to have had a chance like this."

"Well, you and Alex certainly lit up the stage during that last performance! The chemistry was sizzling," Perkins says. "But we hear a rumor he bats for the other team, if you know what I mean. Any romance going on for you two?"

"Not with each other, no." I'm not going there. "Thanks for caring to interview me." I get ready to bolt.

"Well, we heard you have a little something going on with one of the producers of the show: Brandon Forbes." I start walking. Rosa is still following. How did she hear about that? Brandon and I kept things so secret—only Alex knows, or so I'd hoped.

"I can't comment on that," I say, and break into a run.

I don't care how it looks. I can't take another minute of this. Fortunately, the direction I'm headed is toward the front of the hotel, and I duck into the lobby, trying to bring down my breathing—but just inside are more reporters, filling the lobby's lounge area. My rapid entrance attracts them, and they surge up out of the seating arrangements like a pack of wolves, snapping questions at me.

I flee to the stairwell again. Two flights up, I sink onto the tread of one of the steps and put my face in my hands.

What a nightmare.

And now I've gone on TV and said I'm signing with Jashon Mummings, which is all I could think of saying, because I can't deal with seeing Brandon again.

I glance at the cheap plastic Swatch on my wrist: a bright round dial marked with Minnie Mouse. Ruby and Peter bought it for me today at Disneyland, back when life seemed filled with happiness and possibilities. Was that really just today?

It's time for my meeting with Mummings in the hotel bar. I meant to talk to Brandon, see if he was still willing to sign me, and then blow off Mummings. But when I opened the door...My brain mercifully short-circuits the memory of Brandon and Pearl together.

I wonder what Magnus will do to Brandon when he finds out about them, and suppress a quiver of worry. Magnus has never been anything but sweet to me, but I can feel an otherness about him that speaks to having been places and done things that it's better not to know about.

Pearl and Magnus, and their relationship, are not my problem.

Brandon is.

Was.

Isn't any more.

I have to move forward into a life without Brandon in it.

The thought makes me double up with pain. Even if I

somehow misunderstood the situation with Pearl, Brandon wasn't able to answer that question I had for him in the elevator... and I can't hitch my wagon to that uncertain of a star.

At least I'm not a virgin anymore. I can have sex, even with my OCD, if I like the guy enough. Maybe it's worth all of this to know that.

I want to vomit from the pain, but I have to keep it together. I refocus with difficulty.

That gangster-looking Mummings dude is now my best chance for success, and I need to be looking out for myself. I'm the only one who can.

I stand up, every muscle heavy as lead, and squirt some hand sanitizer onto my palms. Thirteen gestures later, I head back down to the lobby.

Jashon Mummings is waiting for me.

CHAPTER TWENTY-TWO

Jade

Jashon Mummings has a woman with him. I want to be reassured by that, but she's just as scary as he is: tight buzz cut hair, huge hoop earrings and a leather bustier are all I can see above the banquette. She reminds me of Grace Jones: shiny brown skin, dark lipstick, and hard eyes.

Mummings stands to greet me, though, bald head shiny in the low light, his double-breasted suit with the red silk kerchief in the pocket sending a message of money—but the giant diamond on his finger speaks of ill-gotten gains.

"Jade. You were amazing last night." He has a voice like coffee grounds—dark and bitter.

"Thanks. I didn't win, though."

"Doesn't matter. You have huge talent, and now the world knows that. Please, sit down. This is Madalyn, my associate." He gestures to the woman, who doesn't smile but does incline her head. Associate? What does that mean?

"Pleased to meet you both." I fold my hands tight in my lap to keep from having to use my sanitizer. "I can only stay a few minutes. I'm super tired from the show."

"Yes, I imagine." Mummings takes a fat envelope out of his breast pocket and sets it on the table. The waitress arrives, and he and Madalyn order drinks. I order a ginger ale, not willing to chance getting carded.

"You an alcoholic?" Madalyn purrs.

"No. Just underage."

Mummings pats the envelope. "Take a look."

I open the envelope. The pages of the contract document are thick with legalese and I can feel my eyes, already gritty and sore, crossing as I try to read the unfamiliar language. "I'm going to need to take this back to my room and study it. Have a lawyer look at it." Ruby can review it and make sure it's okay.

"No need for all that." Mummings takes out another envelope. "Since you didn't win, here's a little pre-payment walking around money. To help you get set up in your own place here in LA."

I peek into the envelope. It's thick with hundred dollar bills. Just holding it makes me nervous. I push it back to him. "Why don't you just—tell me more about what your business, what you have in mind."

"Music videos." He has a gold filling that winks when he smiles. "It's all the thing, and you've got moves."

I'm excited by this. After all, I learned to dance hip-hop by watching MTV videos. "Do you have a team of dancers? Or do you hire individual freelancers?"

"We're building our on-staff team at our own studio. I'm moving from skin movies to legit music videos. I might as well tell you that, since you're going to hear it somewhere. Got my start in pornos, but we're not staying there."

I feel my cheeks heat. "Yeah, I wouldn't be interested in that kind of video work."

"Well, not gonna lie—you're gonna have to show some skin and shake that booty—but it's for TV, so you'll always have something on."

"Let me take this contract and review it. I need to sleep on it." I scoop up the first envelope.

He pushes the fat money-filled one toward me. "This is a gift. Just a sample of the kind of money you can make working for me. It's yours, no matter what you decide."

I pause. I'm literally penniless now that I didn't win. I was hoping for the fifty-thousand-dollar prize money to get set up with a place here in LA. If I don't take this money, I have to beg Rafe and Ruby for a ride on the Learjet back to Eureka.

Back to my teeny, tiny circuit from home, to some lame job, to studio, and around again.

I can't fit into that life anymore.

"All right." I take the envelope. "Thanks."

Mummings hands me his card. It's black, with gold lettering spelling out MUMMINGS VIDEO PRODUCTION and a telephone number. "I want that contract signed and behind us because I have a job for you right away. We're doing a Janet Jackson video."

I sit back down in the booth. "Janet Jackson! Really?" I love her music. It would be such a thrill to be in one of her videos.

"Yeah, but we start filming tomorrow. I was hoping to get you into a solo cameo, but with this lawyer business..." He makes a dismissive clicking sound with his mouth.

I just want to get on with my new life and have something to tell my family when they ask me about returning to Eureka with Mom. I want to have something to say to Brandon when I eventually have to face him—as I know I will. He's going to try to explain away the thing with Pearl, and while I don't want to hear it, I *do* want to have something I can say to fend him off—to not have to deal with him anymore.

I just can't handle my emotions around Brandon. Mummings, and his offer, will ensure that I don't have to be around him for work, or anything else.

"All right." I hold out a hand. "Where's your pen?"

Brandon

I've been looking everywhere for Jade. I've even called hotel security to have them find her—and I'm headed for the bar for one last look, and a stiff drink, when Jade walks out of the bar.

Jashon Mummings and his pit viper are right behind her.

Jade freezes when she sees me. Mummings puts a meaty hand on her shoulder and nods in greeting. "Forbes."

"Mummings. Here to steal my best talent?" My heart's pounding—I want to pop that slimy porn king right in his gold-toothed grin. Instead, I bare my teeth in an attempt at humor.

"I make my own decisions. And I've signed with Mr. Mummings." Jade stares at me defiantly. "We're starting work on a Janet Jackson video tomorrow."

That elevator drop happens to my stomach again. "Jade. We have to talk. Privately."

"I don't think we do." Bright red spots burn in her cheeks as she turns to face her new boss. "Thanks again, Mr. Mummings. I'll meet you in the lobby first thing tomorrow morning when I check out."

"See that you do." Mummings points a huge finger at her, cocked like a gun, and winks. The effect is not cheery. He and his woman head for the front door, and Jade brushes past me.

"Jade!" She's slipping away from me again. The ridiculousness of the situation makes me grab her arm in frustration. "Stop. You have to listen. Pearl came up to warn me that you were talking to that sleazeball, nothing more."

"I don't believe that for a minute." Jade won't look at me. She's fumbling in her pocket for the hand sanitizer. "And that sleazeball is my boss now." She wrenches her arm out of my hand. I frown as she slips onto the nearest elevator just as the door closes.

Well, hell.

I don't actually have time to try to reason with that immature, neurotic, stubborn woman right now, because my mother has cancer surgery and I'm going back to New York tomorrow morning to be there for her—something I should have told Jade yesterday, but we were too busy making love to get around to the "my mother has cancer" conversation.

Like with the Mummings contract, I thought we'd have plenty of time to discuss it.

Maybe Jade needs a lesson in how the real world works. Jashon Mummings is just the guy to give it to her. The thought makes my hands ball into fists.

But if she won't trust me the tiniest bit, if she's so paranoid about her own sister that she won't listen to reason—maybe it already was late.

And maybe I don't want to be with someone who has that little trust in me—someone who'd jump to conclusions so easily after a night like we had, refusing to even talk about it. Then, stab me in the back by going over to the competition.

Why did I let myself get involved with another Michaels girl, exactly? My stomach is roiling as I walk into the bar, sit on a stool, and order several shots. I'm on the third one, still trying to wrap my head around the shambles, when Stu joins me.

"Celebrating without me?" One look at my face and he revises that. "Having a wake without me?" He grabs one of my whiskey shots and throws it back. Shudders. "Ugh. Strictly medicinal. What's going on?"

I tell him what I can bring myself to speak about. "Melissa is having cancer surgery day after tomorrow. I have to go back to New York."

"Aw, hell. Your mother always seemed like she was Teflon-coated. My world just tipped a few degrees off-center with that news." Stu pats the counter for a refill. We pound a few more down together.

"One of my best dancers just signed with Jashon Mummings," I mutter into the bowl of peanuts Stu has dragged over to keep us from getting shit-faced too quickly. "The asswipe got to her before I could."

"Jade Michaels?"

"Yeah."

"Ah, hell. He's going to eat a sweet kid like her alive." Stu shakes his head. "Damn shame."

"Jade's not a kid."

"Oh, it's like that, is it?" Stu eyes me shrewdly. "I thought it might be. Shafted by another Michaels girl, you poor bastard."

I punch him in the shoulder—hard. "Screw you." That crack really hurt. I throw a fifty down on the counter and stand up. "Tomorrow's another day, and I gotta pack."

"Hey, I'll keep an eye on her for you. I do camera work for Mummings sometimes. He's moving out of porno into music videos; that rumor is true, so he probably has real work for her at least. Want me to keep an eye on her?"

"Yeah, man." All that booze I drank too fast swishes unsteadily in my belly. "Would you? She's not a kid, but she is...innocent."

"Innocent, huh?" Stu pats me on the shoulder. "I'll offer my videography services at a cut rate to Mummings. And I'll expect you to make up the difference in pay when he takes me up on it."

"It's a deal." I feel a little better. Jade may be diving into the deep end of the pool holding an anchor, but at least Stu can report to me on how fast she hits the bottom. "Keep me posted."

"And good luck with your mom."

"We both need that." I wave as I walk through the lobby, trying not to weave. Finally reaching the room, I throw my clothes into my suitcase.

What an ignominious end to the best show we've run in three years.

Everything reminds me of being with Jade—the table and chairs where we shared dinner that first evening. The shower. The bed.

I can't even look at it, let alone lie on it.

I set up an early morning wake-up call for my flight to New York—then drink most of the hotel room's wet bar and pass out on the couch.

CHAPTER TWENTY-THREE

Jake

ALEX IS PACKING WHEN I finally reach the sanctuary of our room.

"Where've you been, girl?" Alex smiles archly. "But never mind. I know where. You been doin' the nasty with Mr. Producer."

"Man, are you behind the times." I drag my sorry butt into the bedroom. Trailing after me, folding one of his pairs of shiny hip-hop pants, Alex frowns.

"Come to think of it, you aren't looking so hot. What's happening?"

"Mr. Producer. That's over. A mistake." I pull my backpack, all I came with and now all I'm leaving with, out of the closet. "I signed with Mummings. We start work tomorrow on a Janet Jackson video."

"Wait. What?" Alex cocks a hip, scowling. "How'd you go from hearts and flowers, on top of the world, to signing with Mummings and I don't want to talk about it?"

"Please." I flop on the end of the bed. "Please, Alex. I

can't talk about it right now." The tears I've been holding in since that wretched moment I opened Brandon's door finally overflow. "Don't ask me about it." I dash them off my cheeks. "I wonder if you want to keep being my roommate, though." I pull the cash envelope out of my pocket. "Do you have plans here in LA? Or are you going back to the Bay Area?"

Alex sits beside me. Takes the envelope. Pulls the money out. Whistles as he counts. "That's twenty C-notes right there. Two thousand dollars. What'd he want you to do for that?"

"Nothing. It was a gift."

Alex snorts. "Gift, my left nut. Guy's a porn king gangster."

I snatch the envelope back. "He had beautiful manners and a woman with him when we met. And now I have money to get a place. So do you want to go in on it with me? Because I'll ask around for another roommate if not."

"Course I want to. I need a crib down here too."

"That's a relief." I flop back on the bed. "At least one thing is going right."

Alex loans me a sleeping pill, and I escape into oblivion.

It seems like moments later when the phone on the bedside table rings and jangles me awake the next morning. I'm afraid to answer it in case it's reporters or Brandon. "Can you get that?" I yell at Alex through the open door.

"Chicken." Alex rolls his eyes, but picks up the phone. "Hello?" He listens for a moment. "Yeah, Jade is here." He covers the receiver. "It's your sister Ruby."

I pick up the bedside extension. "Ruby." Just saying her name makes my eyes prickle up as I think of all I'm not telling her, and she's not going to like that I signed a contract without consulting her. "What's going on with the family today?"

"Oh, we're getting ready to go back up North. Pearl and Magnus already checked out. Pearl wasn't feeling well."

Pearl left without even trying to talk to me. *What, just so I could yell at her and show her the door?* Probably. Still, it hurts.

I'm so full of crap. I hate myself.

"I thought Pearl would tell you her news herself, but she said you guys had a misunderstanding." Ruby says.

"Yeah, we did." All I'm not telling Ruby hangs on the tip of my tongue but I bite down on it. "What's this big news?"

"She's pregnant. That's why she hasn't been joining us for meals—she's had to lie down a lot. She wanted to wait until three months to tell people, but decided you should know." Ruby's voice sounds puzzled. "I wish you guys would just get over whatever this problem is between you."

I cover my eyes with a hand as the world shifts.

Do I really think my pregnant sister Pearl, who by every indication is in love with her husband, was trying to seduce Brandon?

I jumped to conclusions. Of course I did. I am such an idiot. *Imbecile is more like it.* Shame rolls over me in a damp greasy fog.

"Oh, that's great," I say faintly.

"Well, Pearl seemed pretty upset. Wouldn't tell me what was wrong so I assume the same old shit?" Ruby sounds annoyed. "Because it's time for you two to bury the hatchet. Speaking of, we're rolling out of here by noon and taking Mom back up to Eureka. You coming?"

"Thanks, sis, but I'm staying here in LA. I signed with a company, and we start work on a music video today, in fact. Speaking of, I need to get ready." I roll out of bed.

"Oh really?" Ruby's voice perks up. "I'm so glad something worked out. It seemed pretty anticlimactic to just have to go straight home. Did you sign with Forbes Talent? I'm hearing Brandon Forbes's new agency is the hottest thing in town."

"No. I went with a different outfit. Mummings Video Production."

"That doesn't sound like an agency."

I blow out a breath. "Listen, thanks, Ruby, but I'm making my own decisions now, and I saw a good thing and hopped on it. I'll be fine. Alex is going to be my roommate, so I won't be alone. I'll give you a call when I'm settled. So tell Mom bye and love, will you?" I'm trying to pull on some dance gear one-handed.

"Tell her yourself," Ruby snaps, and hands the phone to Mom.

"Jade?" Mom's voice sounds worried. "You okay, honey? I can't help overhearing—you've got some work and you're staying down here?"

I repeat everything I told Ruby. "And I have to meet the producer down in the lobby at eight a.m., so I have to run, Mom. I'll be in touch as soon as I have an address. And a phone."

"Honey. You have to give me a hug goodbye." Mom's voice is definite. "I'm coming to your room now."

I sigh as she hangs up. I'm a terrible daughter and sister, but there's no time to wallow, especially if I'm going to have time to go by Brandon's room and apologize for my stupidity before I meet Mummings in the lobby. I crank into gear, brushing and braiding my hair, pulling on dance clothes, zipping up my backpack. "You're going to start looking for apartments today, right?" I call to Alex.

"Sure am, chica. Way ahead of you." Alex waves a newspaper with ads circled in red. "Ernesto and I are going by some of these."

"Ernesto? What? I thought you broke up with him."

"I did. Doesn't mean I'm going to turn him down when he offers to help."

"What's Ernesto doing now that the show's over?"

"Well, he and Selina signed with Forbes Talent, like I did. Today all the dancers who signed with Forbes have a meeting with the coordinator, Chad Wicke, to develop portfolios." Alex folds the newspaper with sharp, precise movements. "I wish you were with us. It seems like a more logical, organized place to start than driving off to get started on a video with no prep or anything."

"We've chosen different paths. And I don't have time to talk about it. Where's a number I can reach you?"

"I have a pager." He rattles off the digits and I write them on the inside of my arm with the hotel's ballpoint.

"I'll call you when I'm done, hopefully we can go look at some apartments," I say. "I have to run." I give Alex a quick hug.

Mom, along with Rafe, Ruby and Peter, are just getting off the elevator. I glance worriedly at my Swatch—it's seven twenty. I'll barely have a half-hour to make up with Brandon before I have to get back to the lobby.

Hugs all around, kisses and well wishes, and the family invites me to have breakfast downstairs in the caf one last time. "Can't. I have to see someone and then meet my ride downstairs at eight a.m.," I tell them. "I'll get a pager today so you guys can contact me. It might be a little while until Alex and I nail down an apartment and get a phone set up."

"Sounds good. Where's that contract you signed with Mummings? Let me give it a quick skim," Ruby says.

"Oh, darn, I left it in the room," I lie. Actually it's in my backpack, along with the fat envelope of cash. "I'll mail you a copy."

"I insist." Ruby wags her finger at me. "I would feel so much better if you'd signed with Forbes Talent."

"Well, I didn't, and now I have to go." I hold Mom extra tight. "You going to be okay without me?"

"Sure, honey. Just call me every week or so, okay?" Mom's hazel eyes look worried, and I touch her cheek.

"Definitely."

We all get on the elevator and I get off a couple floors down, at Brandon's level, with a final round of kissing and waving.

My heart is a drumbeat in my ears as I walk the short distance to Brandon's door, mentally rehearsing my speech. I'm sorry I over-reacted. I was an idiot. Clearly I have some issues I have to work on with my sister, and I'm planning to do that...

I stand in front of Brandon's door and knock.

Knock again.

And again.

No answer.

Maybe he's sleeping, or went to the studio early. I can leave him a note.

I still have my key. I slip it into the lock, push down on the handle.

No one's inside.

There's an empty feeling, like everything that brought life to the room is gone. As I walk to the bedroom I realize there's no sign of anyone occupying the room—the bathroom counter is bare. The chair where he'd thrown a few shirts is empty. I peek into the closet—empty hangers rattle on the rod.

"He's checked out," I murmur. "Oh my God."

I have no way of getting ahold of him. I know he lives in Boston when he's not in LA, but I don't have a phone number, an address, anything.

I find myself counting the furniture as I head for the door.

Down in the lobby, I ask to leave Brandon a message. "That guest has checked out," the receptionist says.

"Is he coming back?" I look around wildly. Why would he have left so quickly? Doesn't the show have to wrap up and do post-processing for a few more days?

I spot Stu the cameraman coming off of one of the elevators, his lanky body curved into an apostrophe. "Stu!" I hurry over to him, even as I spot Madalyn, Mummings's intimidating associate, by the door. "Where's Brandon?"

"Thought you dumped his ass." Stu's eyes are cold. "Dude left for New York."

"Oh, no." I cover my mouth with a hand, my stomach plummeting. "It was a misunderstanding!"

"Well, he had urgent biz in the Big Apple, so that's where he is."

Madalyn approaches, resentment that she has to pick me up plain on her face. "Time to go."

"Hey, I was going to check with your outfit. See if you need any camera guys now that this gig wrapped," Stu says.

"Nope. We've got the camera work covered." Madalyn grabs my arm and tugs me toward the door. Stu narrows his eyes, hands on his hips, as Madalyn tows me through the rotating doors and out into the rest of my life.

Brandon

Mom looks beautiful even with her hazel eyes bare of makeup and trembling lips. She has a death grip on my hand. I pat her soft, springy golden-blonde hair. It's all going to fall out when she has chemotherapy, up next in the horrors planned after this surgery.

She's going to hate losing her hair. I feel so helpless to make anything better for her.

"It's going to be okay, Mom. This is just a lumpectomy— they're not taking off the whole breast."

"But they will, if there's more cancer in there. And they won't know until they get in there if there is."

It's hard for me to see Mom this way: fragile, agitated, her fingers plucking at the patterned hospital gown. Repeating catechisms of reassurance isn't what she needs right now. "I love you, Mom. No matter what. I love you."

She turns her face into my shoulder and squeezes me hard.

Ah. That was what she needed to hear.

Makes me wonder if things might have gone differently if I'd had the courage to say those words to Jade. The cold knife of how things ended with her sticks me in the gut for the hundredth time.

The anesthesiologist arrives. Takes Mom's blood pressure. Hooks up her already-installed IV to a bag of something clear and dripping. Mom pulls herself together and lies back, queenly and composed.

"I'll see you on the other side, son." She smiles, and it feels like a gift, hard-won and precious.

I give that gift back, kissing her hand as I let it go. "I'll be here."

The hours while she's in surgery tick past slowly. I pace the waiting room, looking out the gray glassed-in windows at the jagged teeth of the city's skyline. I thumb through dog-eared copies of National Geographic and People. Mom's two close friends, Katya and Bittie, hold down a couch on the other side of the waiting room but I'm too restless to make conversation with them.

Eventually I go find a pay phone and check in with my director, Alan Bowes.

Everything's on track at the studio. The video team is editing; the dancers have dispersed. A quick call to Chad Wicke tells me he's building the new dancers' portfolios and already has interest from some advertising agencies for using them in a campaign.

Every minute of every long distance call that's going on my gold MasterCard is just a time-filler. The only person I really want to talk to right now, when I'm hurting and sad about Mom, is Jade.

Finally, I call Stu's pager. I save it for last because I know I'm going to have to find a way to ask about Jade without seeming to.

He calls the pay phone back promptly. "This is Brandon. How's the wrap from the cameraman end of things?"

"You called to ask me that? More importantly—how's your mom doing?"

"She's in surgery. I'm going nuts here." I blow out a breath and run a hand through my hair.

"And since I know what you're really calling about—Mummings didn't hire me. And Jade was looking for you this morning. Said you had a 'misunderstanding.' Seemed upset."

"She did?" Hope, igniting in my chest, feels painful.

"Yeah. Seemed like she wanted to get in touch with you."

I don't have a number for Jade if she's left the hotel, and she doesn't have my pager number. Besides, she chose this path. Maybe she needs to go down it awhile.

"Thanks for the update, but Jade's on her own. I'll be back out in LA in a week or so. Thanks for trying to get in with Mummings."

I hang up, and I still don't feel good about the situation.

CHAPTER TWENTY-FOUR

Jade

Mummings's studio is a drafty metal warehouse on the seedy outskirts of Hollywood, well past the boutiques and glitzy lights and deep into wino country. Floodlights are set up on one end, and the air is thick with the smell of marijuana. Mummings is seated in a canvas chair beside the main camera on a big stand near a boom box churning out Top Forty tunes at high volume.

He's only using half the space. The other half is piled with boxed TVs, microwaves and other appliances that have a look about them of having "fallen off a truck", as Mom used to describe stolen items. The main set is a red satin bedroom, probably recycled from Mummings's porn flicks.

Madalyn leads me over to Mummings. "Fetched the kid like you asked."

"Good." He rakes my dancewear with a glance. "I'll send you to wardrobe for the shoot."

"Tell me about the project, Mr. Mummings," I say, firming my voice. "I need to know what I'm doing."

"Jashon. Mr. Mummings is my dad." He smiles, unexpectedly charming. "Well, in the video Janet's singing. She'll be lip-synching and dancing around, and we're filming her at a more upscale location. Her soundtrack is going through the whole video, and what you're going to be doing is the cut scenes that we flash in and out of. A sexy love story."

I stare at the bed. "How sexy?"

Mummings gives a bark of laughter. "Sexy. But like I said, geared for TV. You know your partner for the scene. You two can spend today limbering up with our choreographer." He barks into a handheld walkie for Wilkins and Ferroe.

My eyes widen as David Wilkins, the blond Adonis I danced with early in the dance competition, appears with a petite black woman in tow. "David! Great to see a familiar face!"

David grins at the sight of me, too. "Great to be working with you again."

Diana Ferroe, the choreographer, is a powerhouse. She has the script all mapped out and begins working with us intensively. As soon as I'm dancing and moving, rehearsing the scene, my self-consciousness falls away and nervousness about the big red satin bed fades.

This is legit. This is dancing for a Janet Jackson video. I didn't need to worry about some other agenda.

It's nine p.m. by the time we're ready to wrap for the day. I cover up my dance gear with a big sweatshirt and call Alex's pager from Mummings's old dial phone plugged into the wall, and he hits me back promptly. "Did you make any progress on finding an apartment?"

"No, but I have a bunch for us to visit. Come back to the hotel and crash with me tonight. I took a cheaper room at the same place."

"Great." I'm thrilled to have company and a safe place to go. The barnlike warehouse building has emptied out, and the shadows and echoes are spooky. "I hate to spring for a cab, but I guess I'll have to."

"No need for that. I can drop you off. It's on the way to my crib." Jashon's gritty voice, right behind me, makes me jump. I turn with a smile.

"Great. Need to get back to the Marriott. Really appreciate it."

I hang up with Alex, relieved that the immediate problem of where to sleep is solved, and turn to Jashon. "I really appreciate it. The only money I have is that gift you gave me, and I don't know when we get paid next, so..."

"So I take it you didn't read your contract carefully." Jashon opens the steel door for me, hits the lights. Darkness drops like a cloak over the great dim warehouse. "You really should have."

I walk just ahead of him toward the dim, bulky shape of a maroon-colored Cadillac parked under the yellow light casting a pool of illumination over the lot. "You saying you tried to pull a fast one on me?" I make my tone light with an effort.

"No. It's just always good to read the fine print." He unlocks the Caddy and opens the door for me.

I slide onto the buttery upholstery of the passenger side. It smells like leather and weed inside, a sweet funk emanating from an overflowing ashtray in the dash.

Jashon gets in, adjusting the black leather trench he's wearing. "We might as well get something to eat on the way."

My stomach, fed by nothing but cups of coffee and a few energy bars provided by a filming assistant, rumbles loudly in agreement with this. "Maybe just a drive-through," I murmur. "If you don't mind. I'm really tired."

"Yeah, Ferroe's giving you two a workout." Jashon seems to be in a good mood, tapping his big gold ring on the steering wheel. The Caddy seems to flow over the road, and I can't hear anything inside but the mellow, smoky jazz he's playing. "We should get to actual filming tomorrow."

"I'm surprised that the love story part of the video is a white girl and guy," I tell him after we've turned into an Arby's drive through and decimated a couple of roast beef sandwiches, still sitting in the car. "I mean, that sounds wrong..."

"No, that's a legit question." Mummings dabs his mouth with a paper napkin. "We're trying to reach out to all audiences. Make this a really mainstream video. We did some market testing, and the broadest appeal is going to combine the best of both worlds. As it were." Mummings keeps surprising me with how sophisticated and intelligent he is. His warm brown eyes flash humor at me. "You'll see. We're going to have a hit on our hands."

"I hope so. David's good. I'm glad you signed him."

"He, at least, read his contract," Mummings pats my leg and squeezes my thigh as he pulls up at the hotel. It's definitely more intimate than I would have liked, but until this minute he's been a perfect gentleman so I let it slide. "Be out here at seven thirty tomorrow morning and Madalyn will pick you up."

"Great. Thanks for the ride." I hop out of the car and pat the roof as he pulls away.

Alex has left a key for me at the main desk and I find my way to a tiny room overlooking the back alley dumpsters.

"My, how the mighty have fallen." I wave my hand in front of my nose as I inhale the smell of old cigarettes embedded in the carpet and drapes. "We've come down in the world."

"What do you want for fifty bucks?" Alex is sprawled on one of two double beds, a fashion magazine open before him. "And we have to find something even cheaper than this."

"I'll have to ask to leave early tomorrow or something. They worked us every minute." I tell him about the experience. "Mummings was cool. He brought me back here and bought me Arby's."

Alex frowns. "Watch out for that guy."

"Everyone's so freaked out about him. So far, it's great. Dancing with David is terrific."

We chat for a while and Alex yawns. "I need my beauty sleep."

"Me too." A quick shower, then into bed.

I don't think of Brandon until I'm there. Lying on my back, I remember him sliding up over me, his lips on mine, my hands all over his hard body. I loved the feeling of his solid thigh between mine, the sound of satisfaction he made as he entered me—the incredible feeling of it, such a sweet, hot invasion.

"Sleep well," Alex says from his side of the room.

"I'll try." I sigh, and wrap my pillow around my head. Sleep takes a while.

Brandon

Mom comes through the surgery well, according to her doctor, a prematurely balding man wearing round, plastic-rimmed glasses he should have ditched in the eighties. "The cancer site was localized. We were able to check all the margins and make sure it hadn't spread. She's missing a significant amount of tissue from that breast, but I set it up for reconstruction which shouldn't be too bad." Katya and Bittie are hugging each other, ready to jump up and down with happiness, but I'm still worried.

"Does she still need chemo?"

"Yes." He flips down the pages of her chart. "We'll schedule the reconstruction after eight rounds of chemo."

So Mom has a rough road ahead. I'd hoped that she wasn't going to need the chemo and lose her hair, but it's not to be.

She's groggy but peaceful when they get her settled in a

room, and after making sure she has everything she needs, including a dozen yellow roses, I leave her with her friends and head to the apartment we keep in the city.

It's a starkly modern place with two small bedrooms but the kind of view and living room area that are meant for parties and seeing and being seen—an ongoing part of Melissa's business, and mine too, come to think of it, though I've always left that part to her.

I have a ton of paperwork and phone calls to catch up on, but I take a moment to dim the lights. I gaze out over the view of a nearby park, a square of green velvet rendered in black and white. Buildings, studded with lights like square candles in uneven rows, lead the eye down to the arterial red glow of taillights from the traffic moving through the streets.

And I wonder where Jade is. What she's doing.

She's before me in my mind's eye, spread out like a banquet, everything about her delicious...I turn away with a curse and head for the shower.

CHAPTER TWENTY-FIVE

Jade

MADALYN PICKS ME UP IN the morning and the day is no less strenuous than the previous one as we begin filming. We do take after take to get the scenes just right. Mummings is hands-on with everything, directing the shoot and having us redo the scenes.

In a way this kind of dance is easier than having to learn a whole piece, because we shoot segments. In another way it's harder, because we have to throw ourselves into these short scenes without any warm-up.

I play a country girl in a flowered dress that swirls and whips around my thighs, tiny buttons all down the front. David is my boyfriend, wearing a tiny black wife-beater tank and battered leather jeans, a heavy wallet chain hitting him in the waist all day. Privately, I think David's too clean-cut for the part, but after they airbrush some tattoos on his neck and arms, he makes it work and there's no doubt the boy can dance.

We go all day, and at a wrap point I ask to get off early. "My roommate and I need to look for a rental. He's got some addresses for us to check out."

"How are you getting around?" Jashon strokes the tiny soul patch on his chin as he narrows his eyes at me.

"Don't know. Taxis? Maybe the bus?" We don't have wheels yet. Another major obstacle to find a way over.

"You can use the company car." He digs a set of keys out of his pocket. "The one Madalyn picked you up in. It's outside. Bring it back tomorrow morning."

"Thanks, Jashon!"

He smiles then, a slow hook of the mouth. "Gimme some sugar." And he taps his lips.

My eyes widen. I glance around but everyone seems busy, not paying attention. "I don't know..."

"Oh come on, baby girl." He taps his lips again, smiling. "You scared?"

This is my boss, and he just loaned me the car. So I lean in and give him a peck on the lips—and he lets it go at that, though I see something in his eyes that I realize he's been hiding the whole time, a certain heat that makes me pull back quickly. I can feel his eyes on my butt as I walk across the studio, waving to David, and out to the car. It's a big, solid black Buick. I think I can remember the way back to the hotel, and wish I had a map.

As if reading my mind, Madalyn appears and taps on the window of the Buick. I roll down the window and she hands me a book, her mouth pulled into a disapproving pucker. "Jashon told me to loan you this." It's a small road atlas of Los Angeles.

"Oh, thank you!" I gush, but she's already walking away. She definitely doesn't like me.

Alex is suitably impressed with my wheels, and we spend the remaining daylight hours visiting a series of seedy rentals. We finally settle on a two-bedroom a few blocks over from Sunset

Boulevard, choosing it because it has a pool (green with algae) and blinds already in place.

It's also completely bare of furniture, so after I use cash to secure the place, we make our way to a nearby Walmart and buy blow-up air mattresses and some basics from a thrift store. By the time we finish that up with a trip to the grocery store, I'm anxiously counting my cash.

"I'll reimburse you my half as soon as I get paid," Alex says. "We're gonna be fine."

"I really do need to read my contract," I tell him. "But I'm so tired. Tomorrow."

We blow up the mattresses and sleep the sleep of the truly exhausted on our air mattresses after I get all the secondhand bedding washed. With my germ phobia, there's no way I can sleep on anything used. Still, I wake up several times during the night, battling the feeling that creepy-crawlies are getting on me. I eventually have to get up and set my bed in the exact middle of the room, the cardboard box holding my sparse clothing in one corner, the backpack in another. On my back, counting the ceiling tiles in the dim streetlights reflecting through the cheap blinds, I think of all the unfinished business I still have to do.

Get a phone line ordered for the apartment.

Get my own pager so people can tag me.

Get ahold of Mom and let her know I'm okay.

Reconcile with Pearl.

Call Brandon and see if he'll give me another chance.

CHAPTER TWENTY-SIX

Jade

I GET UP EXTRA EARLY THE next morning and call Mom from the pay phone od the corner.

"It's so great to hear your voice," I tell Mom. "We're doing good. Already found our own apartment, and it has a pool." I like how nice that sounds even if the reality is a scummy hole I'm afraid to dip a toe in for all the germs. "On today's to-do list is getting a pager and a phone line. I'll let you know as soon we have those. Hey, listen, I need to get ahold of Pearl. Do you have her number?" I accidentally on purpose lost the slip of paper Brandon gave me with her number on it.

"Of course." Mom seemed oblivious to the silence between Pearl and I, and I hope she never knows of it. She rattles off Pearl's number and I write it on my arm with a ballpoint. I scan the empty street—no one around still, though dawn is beginning to bleed up from behind the buildings. It's going to be several hours later in Boston, where Pearl lives.

Using the last of my quarters, I call my sister. Her voice, answering, is thick with sleep. "Hello?"

"Pearl? It's Jade. I'm sorry to wake you up."

"No problem." I hear the rustle of bedding as she sits up. "I should have been up hours ago, but I've been so tired lately."

"Yeah. About that. I heard your news from Ruby. Congratulations."

"It was a surprise. But we're happy about it." I can hear in her voice that she really is happy about it. "So. Are you calling about that...situation with Brandon?"

"Exactly." I blow out a breath, winding the metal phone cord around my finger. "I'm sorry I jumped to the wrong conclusion. It wasn't fair to you. Or him."

"Well, I'm glad you finally started thinking clearly." Pearl's voice strengthens as she gets more indignant. "I'm so over Brandon it's not even funny. Magnus is my husband. He's everything to me. I never even did anything but kiss Brandon. And that was four years ago. I can't believe you think he still has a thing for me when he's so clearly hooked on you."

"I don't know what to say." I drift into silence. The news that they never did more than kiss settles in and spreads through me slowly, warming me up. "I still think he was really into you."

"Yeah, he was, but that was a long time ago. Please. Whatever this comparison thing is that you've got going on with me—I wish you'd let it go. I love you. You're my sister. I want us to be friends."

"Me too, Pearl." I feel stronger now that I'm standing on my own two feet. Paying rent with my own money. Signing my own contracts with gangsters. Ruining my own relationships. "I really appreciated you and Magnus coming to support me during the show."

"It was so exciting! A real pleasure. So what are you doing now that it's over?"

"I've signed with a video production company and just today

Alex and I rented an apartment." I sketch out what's been happening. "So far it's going great."

"Well, you have my number. Call me if you need anything."

"And I'll let you know when we get our phone put in. Bye, Pearl. Love you."

I end the call.

Pearl's my sister and wants to be my friend. She never did anything more than kiss Brandon. Whew. I'm so relieved.

Now I need to get ahold of Brandon, but I have no idea how.

Alex might know.

I trot back across the road to our building, noticing a pair of hunched, dark shapes in a nearby alley lighting up. Yeah, apparently it's never too early in the day to start using here in LA. Back in our apartment, Alex is just waking up.

"Get up, sleepyhead. I need to call Brandon Forbes." I prod him with my toe. "It's past time."

"Well, I don't have his digits." Alex grumbles, rolling to the side and getting up. "But I guess you can call the agency number and leave a message. He's still in New York, according to Chad."

"Why did he take off for New York like that? I thought the show would take a few days to wrap."

"Apparently there's a family emergency. I couldn't get any details from Chad, but it's something involving his mother."

"The famous Melissa?"

"The very one."

I go to my room and dress for the day, worried and upset. Not only did I overreact—but Brandon was going through some health emergency with his mom, and I wasn't there for him. If possible, I feel even worse about the situation.

Alex hands me a business card. "Write the number down somewhere. I need that card back."

I add the Forbes Talent Agency's number to the collection on my arm, high up near the elbow where it's out of danger of being washed off. I hand the card back to Alex. "Need a ride some-where while I still have wheels?"

"Sure. You can drop me off at the agency building."

"He has a building already?"

"Forbes already had a business, remember. He just added on the talent agency."

Using the atlas, we navigate our way to a glossy bronze high-rise not far from the studio area. "Still think you should have signed with Mummings?" Alex grins, gesturing to the upscale building.

I shake my head. "I'm the one driving a company car."

"Just make sure that's all you end up driving."

"Oh, stuff it." But at the same time I feel a quiver of appre-hension, remembering the look in Jashon's eyes. "I can handle myself."

Alex slams the door and waves, heading into the sleek build-ing. As I merge back into traffic and take a turn for the worse, I wonder again if I signed with the right outfit.

The day is long, again, but I find time on a lunch break to borrow the car and go to Radio Shack to buy a pager. I've never had one before. It feels so exciting to have a way that people can contact me directly. At the checkout, I count my remaining cash. It's really time to figure out when I get paid next.

CHAPTER TWENTY-SEVEN

Brandon

I STRETCH MY LEGS AS BEST I can under the seat ahead of me and wriggle my shoulders back, knocking into the elderly lady beside me, whose cottony coif is just the right height to be crushed by my shoulder.

"Sorry," I say for the fourth or so time.

She pats my arm. "I like a man with a nice set of shoulders."

I pat her arm back. "Thank you, ma`am."

I'm reduced to being flirted with by octogenarians.

We're finally circling into LA, and there's some delay in the air. This was one of those ungodly early flights that was supposed to put me in early enough in the day to do some business, but with one thing and another it's going to be four by the time I get to the office. I tug the sleeve of my jacket down over my Breitling so I don't see it, lean my head back, and shut my eyes as the plane circles the airport.

Melissa, recovering at home after discharge, seemed to sense the agitation I was trying to hide as I fetched her a glass of water for her pain pill. "What's bothering you, son?"

Much of the stiffness between us has fallen away through this crisis, and through her opening her hand to give me the talent part of the business. I no longer feel so defensive around her, like I have to keep asserting myself.

I can just love her now, and instead of resisting that, she seems to be enjoying it just as much as I am.

But the thing with Jade *is* eating at me. I can't stop thinking about her.

"I met someone," I find myself saying. Not since Pearl have I said a word to Melissa about who I'm dating. Something told me, after that relationship, that I was better off keeping quiet on the subject—not that there has been anyone but transient company.

"That's good." Mom's gaze on mine is straightforward. "I've had time to think, through this whole experience. In hindsight, I've not been as supportive of you in that area as I should have been. As I would like to be, in the future."

I don't know what she's referring to, exactly, but I'll take it. "Thought no one would ever be good enough for you, Mom." I blunt the edge of the comment with humor.

She shrugs, smiling sadly. "I want you to be happy. And I don't think you're happy, alone. At least I had your father for the time I had him."

"And you should date again, too, Mom." I've been wanting to tell her that for a while.

"You think I haven't?" She smiles. "There's a lot you don't know about me, sonny boy, and we're going to keep it that way. But take this to the bank and cash it: life is short. Don't miss out on love, if you find you have a chance at it."

Love? Is that what I feel for Jade?

Not yet. Not now. But given half a chance, I know it could be.

The plane lands at last, and I bid my cute seatmate goodbye, retrieve my bag, and take a cab to the office. As always, walking up to the smooth, modern building lifts my energy and gives me a sense of excitement. And now I'm adding a whole new dimension to my work there.

Kerry meets me outside my office. "Boss, Chad Wicke is inside, waiting for you. Says he needs space to work."

"I rent three offices on this floor. Why didn't he just move into one?" The erstwhile photographer and current creative manager of Forbes Talent must be frustrated by me being out of town.

"Where, Boss? Exactly." We discuss the overcrowding for a moment. I issue a stream of directions and phone calls for her to make. Chad opens the door of my office.

"Finally," he says. Chad's decked out in tailored black pants, wingtips, and a lime green button-down. "Thought you'd be here an hour ago."

"Plane was delayed. We're trying to get you space to work. Kerry's on it. Now what else is going on with our brand-new agency?"

"Let me get you up to speed."

I follow him into the office and flop, with a grunt of relief, into the leather office chair that belonged to my dad. I've lugged that chair to every place I've worked since Mom gave it to me after college. Chad and I get caught up and then I work around to my hidden agenda. "Got any way to get ahold of Jade Michaels? I'm still hoping to sign her."

"I think it's too late. I hear from her roommate, Alex Rodriguez, that she's already working more than full-time with Mummings Video Production."

"Yeah, I know, but I'm hoping to lure her away. The girl's got potential, and just like her sister, tons of charisma."

"I agree. I've got a pager number for Alex. You want it?"

It's probably the only way I'll be able to get ahold of her. "Sure."

Chad checks a little black address book and rattles it off. I make a note, fold it, tuck it in my pocket. "Well, I think we've both worked hard enough today. Kerry's looking for additional space on this floor for the agency to rent and you'll be in there. I'm having her look for an assistant for you, too. So let's reconvene and get right to it tomorrow."

"Sounds good."

Chad leaves, I dismiss Kerry once her phone calls for the new office rental are done, and I dial Alex's pager number and leave my digits. I'm sure he'll call me back, because this is the office number Chad Wicke has been using.

I sit back, prop my feet on the desk, interlace my fingers over my belly, and indulge in a daydream about Jade while I wait for Alex to call me back.

I'm just getting to the good part of the daydream, the part where Jade wraps her legs around me and whispers, "Yes," in my ear, when the phone rings. I drop my feet to the ground with a curse and pick up. "Forbes."

"Mr. Forbes? I thought this was Chad calling." Alex sounds surprised.

"No, I called you. I'm looking for a way to contact Jade. Jade Michaels."

"Oh. Well. We're roommates. She's here in the apartment. Asleep."

I like thinking of Jade, asleep. Maybe even naked, and asleep.

I shake my head—I'm really cranked up. "I'd like a way to contact her. If you have one."

"I'm not sure she'd want me to give out that info." Alex's voice is hesitant. "I'll give her your number to call you back, okay?"

"Sure, I understand." My tone is over hearty, because I'm disappointed even while I respect his decision to let Jade choose to contact me. "That's fine. Tell her I want to discuss...her contract." It's the only thing I can think of at the moment.

"Will do. And may I say—thanks for the opportunity?" Alex's voice waxes enthusiastic. "Chad is great. Ernesto, Selina and I are psyched to be working for your agency."

"No. I work for *you*," I tell him. "That's how an agency operates. We hustle work for you, you go and do the work, you get paid through us, and we take a cut. It's a win-win. But I'm worried that Jade doesn't have as good a situation."

"You're right to be worried!" Alex spills the situation with Jade's contract: indentured servant wages, and huge restrictions. "She didn't read the contract. But she's working with her sister to get it changed."

"I certainly hope so. Please tell her to call me. I'm sure we can help." I say goodbye and hang up. Waiting for her to call might not be good enough.

My fists clench. That sleazebag Mummings did just what I was afraid he'd do.

Jade

My new pager beeping wakes me in the morning. I grab it off the floor beside my blow-up mattress and recognize Ruby's number. "Oh, good." I crawl out of the secondhand sleeping bag, knuckle the sleep out of my eyes in the bathroom, and throw on clothing.

Alex's door is closed, so I tiptoe through the apartment and hurry down the stairs, exiting the building. Dawn in LA is the soft gray and pink tones of a dove's breast, and the sleazy feel of the street is gone now that a trash pickup and street sweeper had been at work—and the night dwellers have gone to their daytime lairs. A few cars are meandering down the street as I cross it to the pay phone.

It's already hours later on the east coast, so Ruby must have had time to work on my contract.

"This is a terrible contract," Ruby says. "I can't believe you didn't let me have a look at it when I was there."

"I know it's bad. Can you fix it?" I'm counting the cement squares of the sidewalk around the phone as I rub sanitizer into my hands, the hand piece of the phone covered with a piece of tissue where it's pressed to my ear.

"I can. But don't go in to the studio today. Tell Mummings your lawyer won't let you return to work until you have a meeting. In the meantime, I'm taking the Lear out. Set up a meeting with him for this afternoon."

"He's not going to like it." My hands sweat at the thought of the upcoming conversation. I squirt more sanitizer onto them.

"So? You won't be facing him alone."

"Ruby, thanks so much. I don't know what I'd do without you."

"I'm just glad you finally wised up and called me. See you soon!" She hangs up briskly, presumably to go pack and then sharpen her teeth to take a bite out of Mummings.

Before I can lose my nerve, I call the studio. I sigh with relief when Mummings doesn't answer, and I leave a message that I won't be in until we have a meeting with my lawyer to make changes to my contract. "And if you want to fire me because of this, that's okay," I finish. "I have other offers for work. I'll be in around three p.m. with my lawyer to go over the contract."

I hang up decisively, but my heart's pounding as I trot across the street and back upstairs to the apartment. Coffee's perking when Alex, hair frazzled, slouches out of his room in his boxers.

"Where'd you go?"

"Across the street to use the phone. Ruby called. I'm not

going in to work until she gets here. We're going to meet with Mummings and get my contract amended."

"Sure you don't want to just can it? Brandon Forbes called me late last night. Wanted to talk to you about your contract."

I feel a sensation in my chest like a lead fishing weight dropping to disappear into the muddy bottom of a pond. "Is that all he called about?"

"I don't know." Alex's bright brown eyes on my face seem to see too much. "He wanted you to call. Left his number. Said it was to talk to you about your contract. He asked for your number, too, but I didn't want to give it out without checking with you first."

"Thanks. I appreciate that."

In the shower, I mull over the situation. *Should I call him?*

No. I want to resolve this situation with Mummings first, solve it myself—and then I can see if Brandon's interest in me is purely professional—or if it's personal.

If it's professional, after I deal with Mummings, I'll be in a better position to negotiate a good contract with Forbes Talent.

If it's personal, not having a contract with Brandon will put me on more equal footing with him.

Alex hands me a scrap of paper with a number on it when I get out. "That's his private phone line," Alex says. "He really seemed to want to hear from you. Gonna call him?"

"Not yet." I fold the paper and slip it into my purse.

"Don't wait too long. He'll move on," Alex cautions. I know he's talking about both the personal and the professional.

I shrug like it doesn't matter. "Got things to work out first."

I take a taxi to meet Ruby at the airport in the private jet area, and the attendant lets me inside the high chain-link fence. Ruby gets off the sleek white jet wearing a black double-breasted suit with a pencil skirt that showcases her terrific legs. Her red hair is tamed into a smooth roll at the back of her head, and Pearl is following. Pearl looks amazing even in the jeans and sweatshirt she's wearing, and I feel my spirits lift at the sight of the two of them.

"You both came!"

"Wouldn't have missed a chance to see you," Pearl says. Holding her in a close hug, I realize how seldom I have ever done that. Time to change all that.

Ruby's green eyes flash with the light of battle—she's eager to get to Mummings. "I hope you told the taxi to wait."

"I did." I embrace her, careful not to mess up her hair. "Thanks so much for doing this, Ruby."

"What are sisters for?" Ruby holds me at arm's length and looks me over. "Good wardrobe choices."

Like her, I dressed to send a message that I mean business today. I'm in a pair of black tailored slacks and a silk blouse, both from the Goodwill but freshly washed. I have on square-toed alligator pumps that pinch but will keep me alert, and add a couple inches to my height.

"We should just get to his studio by three," I tell my sisters as we get into the taxi I told to wait at the curb. "Perfect timing."

We spend the drive to the studio reviewing the documents she's prepared and strategizing. "I'm coming too," Pearl says. "He should know what he's getting into if he messes with you—I can seriously mess things up for him with just a few words to the right people in the industry."

"Thanks, Pearl." For once, I not only appreciate Pearl's clout but her willingness to come out swinging in support of me. It makes me sad for all the lost time that I spent resenting her. I clasp her hand. "You don't have to do this."

"But I do," she says. "What are sisters for?"

Getting out in front of the dreary warehouse tattooed with graffiti in a variety of competing gang colors, Ruby frowns with her hands on her hips. "Really? This is it?"

"Jashon films in a better studio uptown too." I find myself defending Mummings. We tell the cab to wait. "We won't be here long." Hopefully.

Inside, Janet Jackson's song thumps in the background as David and some other male dancers, stripped to the waist and spray-tanned, dance a segment that Janet will be inserted into. Mummings is seated in his canvas chair but spots us. He gestures to his assistant to carry on and comes to meet us.

"My office," he says without greeting, but I see by the uneasy flicker of his eyes that he's recognized Pearl. We follow him across the dim space, stepping carefully over exposed cables and around a pile of microwaves to the small, enclosed office at the back.

Mummings turns on an air conditioner, providing welcome circulation, and closes the door behind us. His desk, a battered steel affair, has been cleared off. Two plastic chairs are in front of it. "Sorry, I don't have a third chair," he says.

"I'll stand," Pearl takes a position behind Ruby and me. Even in her casual clothing, she has a bearing like royalty.

"Ruby McCallum-Michaels, Esquire." Ruby extends her hand to Mummings. He shakes it reluctantly.

"And I'm Pearl Michaels. Supermodel." Pearl does not offer a hand to shake.

Jashon Mummings nods to her in acknowledgment. "Pleased to have you in my office."

Ruby goes on. "I represent Jade, and frankly, sir, should have seen this ridiculous contract before she signed it."

"Spare me." Mummings leans forward and makes a pyramid with his thick fingers. "Jade is damn lucky to have steady work. Any dancer would be lucky to kick off her career in a Janet Jackson video."

"That may be the industry standard in Los Angeles—indentured servant wages and squalid working conditions—but I'm familiar with the union standards for dancers, here and in New

York, and they're a considerable step up from what you're offering."

He and Ruby spar for several moments, taking each other's measure. Finally, Mummings sits back, lacing his fingers over his belly. He's wearing a neon yellow silk button-down with a wide, pointed collar that should look ridiculous but somehow doesn't, contrasting richly with his skin tone and tailored slacks. His shaved head gleams under the harsh lights as he leans forward, locking eyes with Ruby again. "What's your proposal?"

"I drafted an amended contract." Ruby opens her calfskin briefcase with assertive clicks of the brass hasps and removes a couple of pages printed on heavy vellum. "It's a take-it-or-leave-it proposition."

"I can see by this fancy paper that it is." Mummings takes the contract, and, leaning back, begins to read.

Sneaking a glance at Ruby, I'm impressed with her composure as her calm eyes rest on Mummings. But her jaw is a tight, square line whose stubborn set is reflected in a mouth more used to smiling.

I've always known Ruby had a steel core, but this is my first time seeing it in action. I twist my germy hands in my lap and look down to count the linoleum tiles of the floor. When I reach thirteen, I start over again.

Mummings finally looks up from the pages. "Double the wages? No agency fee? I'm glad you at least gave me first right of refusal of her services."

"Are you an agency? Do you plan to manage Jade's career and find her other work, should you not have any available?"

"No." Mummings looks at the contract again. "I plan to keep her plenty busy myself, though. And if I refuse to sign?"

"We walk. That contract was signed by an underage minor under duress. It's null and void."

"We could argue that in court."

"It would cost you too much to make it worthwhile," Ruby says.

"And I know a few industry folks who would be interested to know what kind of an operation you're running out here," Pearl says.

A long pause. I start counting the ceiling tiles.

"Damn it." Mummings fumbles in a drawer and takes out a pen. He signs the contract with an illegible scrawl and pushes it over to me.

I sign my name beneath his.

"Good." Ruby collects the contract and slips it into her brief-case. "I'll have a copy messengered to you tomorrow. Jade will show up for work tomorrow morning. Come on, Jade." She and Pearl walk out the door.

I stand and look Jashon Mummings in the eye. "This is all strictly business." I hope my double meaning is clear to him. *I won't be tolerating any more touching.*

He snorts and shakes his head. "Can't blame a guy for trying."

"Yes, I can." I smile. "But I hope you're not too pissed about this."

"Anything to get Pearl Michaels in my office, even for five minutes." He smiles, too. "And I should have known better than to tangle with a couple of redheads. Go on, get out of here —but be here bright and early tomorrow, ready to work." He makes a shooing motion with his hand, and the diamond flashes.

Out at the waiting taxi, I hug Ruby and Pearl again. "You were both amazing. I can't believe he signed it. We got everything we asked for."

"Didn't give him much choice, between the legal precedents and Pearl offering to ruin his reputation." Ruby looks at the driver. "Take us to the nearest Kinko's. We need to make some copies, and then on to the airport." The taxi moves out, and she turns to me. "What was that last part about?"

"Mummings got a little personal with me. I wanted to make sure that stopped, too."

"Good for you. Now, I hope you don't mind if we turn the plane right back around and return to Boston. The boys hate me being gone—and frankly, I hate leaving them, too."

"Me too, Jade. I'm just not feeling that well." Pearl looks zapped, like she needs a nap.

"No, that's okay, I totally understand." *Good. I can call Brandon tonight.* My heart hammers at the thought.

CHAPTER TWENTY-EIGHT

Brandon

Alex inserts his key into the door of his and Jade's apartment. "It's not much," he says apologetically. "Hopefully she's home." He pushes the door wide—and Jade comes out of a bedroom. She's wearing a pink silk blouse and black pants. Her hair is pulled back into a knot. She looks gorgeous, and more adult than I've ever seen her.

"Brandon!" She blushes brighter than her blouse. "I was just going down to the pay phone to call you. We don't have a phone put in here yet."

"Well, I'm here," I say. We stare at each other for a long moment. "Can we talk?"

"I'll give you guys some privacy," Alex says. "I can go in my room."

"I have a better idea," Jade says. "Come with me." She walks past, and I smell a tiny whiff of something antiseptic, along with vanilla perfume.

Her hand sanitizer. God, she's adorable. The thought makes me smile as I follow her out, down the hall to an exit door and a set of metal stairs.

"I discovered this yesterday." Jade ascends the stairs ahead of me. She's wearing a pair of alligator pumps that ring on the treads, and those tailored pants drape perfectly over her tight butt. That schoolmarm blouse is tucked in by a leather belt around her waist. I could watch her climb stairs in front of me all day long—but unfortunately, there are only a couple of flights to the roof.

The heavy metal exit door gives her some trouble.

"Let me." I haul that sucker open with a screech.

The roof of the building stretches out before us, warm in the evening, tarpapered with a gravelly surface. A ventilator shaft whirs nearby, and the rack of a massive TV antenna rises like the antlers of a robotic stag. The sun's waning red light plays over windows and outlines of the buildings around us. Far below, sound muffled by distance, the arteries of the city flow both ways, clogged lighted traffic. LA is beautiful in the sunset.

Jade leads me to the waist-high parapet encircling the roof and leans a hip on it. The sunset catches fire in her auburn hair. "I really was just heading out to call you," she says. "I had some business to take care of first."

"Oh yeah?" I rest a hip on the parapet too, facing her. "What business?"

"Dealing with my contract with Mummings. I heard from Alex that you were concerned about it, and I was too. My sisters came out today and helped me get it amended."

"I was concerned about your involvement with him. I wanted to sign you with Forbes Talent from the beginning."

"I know, and there are reasons I wasn't sure that was the right thing for me to do. Is that all you...wanted to talk to me about?" Jade glances up at me through the screen of her lashes. My heart's pounding so hard under my silk shirt that each beat feels like a fist squeezing.

"No. That's not all I wanted to talk to you about," I whisper.

Jade leans toward me, and with no finesse at all, I haul her into my arms, working her body deep into the open space between my thighs. My mouth descends to meet hers, and she gives a perfect, tiny moan as we kiss.

My hands slide over the delicious shape of her, slender and firm, as I settle her as close to me as I can get her. One hand on the back of her head, one at her waist, I mold her body to mine. Our mouths tell a story we can't find words for: *I want you. I need you. I can't get enough of you. You taste and feel so good. I never want to be without you again.*

I love you.

The realization bursts across my brain like a rocket igniting the night sky, but I can't say the words. It's too much, too soon, and I still don't know how she feels about me.

"I missed you," I say instead, into that tender velvety place behind her ear that smells like vanilla.

"I missed you, too. I'm sorry for being so freaky," she says. "I was all wrong about you and Pearl. I'm so ashamed of myself."

"Don't be. Just don't leave me again." And I laugh so I don't sound too intense.

"I won't," she says. "I want you so much."

The hardness pressing against her pelvis must tell her it's mutual.

"Can we—go somewhere?"

"I'll kick Alex out," she says. "I just need you. So bad. Right now."

My whole body clenches at her words, and I think of pushing her up against the rampart and—but no. We need more than that. More privacy, more time.

I can hardly let go of her enough to follow her toward the stairs.

We keep our hands linked. The apartment is mercifully empty when we reach it after a marathon of kissing all the way down the stairs.

I've never felt like this before, every nerve alive and vibrating, every taste of her making me hungrier. She checks that Alex is gone, then opens the door of her room, turning to me with an embarrassed smile. "I'm sorry. I don't have furniture yet."

I bang the door shut with my heel.

"You think I care? I hope you aren't too attached to this." I grab the front of her prim blouse, tug it out of her pants, and rip it open. Buttons fly in all directions to the music of ripping cloth. She gives a cry of surprise—and arousal. Her small, perfect breasts bounce into my hands in their demure white lace cups. Their nipples are peach promises just begging for my mouth. Her eyes meet mine in a fierce blaze of hungry green.

I make them mine, sucking and biting through the fabric, but I hardly have time to really get to know them before she grabs my designer silk shirt in both hands and tears it off too, a dramatic rending that makes me laugh.

"I've dreamed about this chest." She puts her mouth on my nipple, a feeling both electric and hot.

I groan and my erection pulses. "I need to be in you. Please."

"And I need you in me." She grabs my belt buckle, and I hers, and we strip each other, falling onto the humble air mattress on the floor together.

I barely get the condom on and then I'm driving deep into her. She bucks beneath me with a cry, coming apart almost instantly as I sink fully into her. My hands dug into her hips, her shoulders, trying to bring her even closer as I wait out her climax, relishing the feeling of the waves of her clenching around me, her flushed face beautiful before me. Her cries are music, and everywhere smells of vanilla and sex...

Finally, Jade calms, and opens her eyes to gaze into mine.

She tips her hips up and wraps her legs tighter. "More."

The feeling that I have, as I give her that *more*, as I find a rhythm, is of coming home.

Jade

He's going so fast and so hard now that I'm hanging on for dear life: my hands are clenched in the chiseled muscles of Brandon's buttocks, and he's pistoning into me. The air mattress slides with each thrust across the floor and fetches up against the wall, something I might have found funny another day—and still he's not done, his eyes fierce on mine, his hands everywhere, his possession total.

I couldn't love this more: his intensity, the leashed violence of it, the pounding pressure, as if to break me open—but instead it just winds me tighter, takes me higher.

I feel another gathering, a tightening coil low in my belly, the storm of passion building, building, building... about to shatter both of us. It crests inside me, a dizzying fullness, a depth of exquisite, intense sensation, and it pushes me across an invisible threshold.

I ride the edge for just a few seconds more so I can see him climax. His eyes close as his back arches high over me and his face darkens as a hoarse sound is wrenched from his throat—and then I let go.

The hot spiral of feeling explodes through me, cascading lights blinding me as ecstasy ripples through my body, and I match his cry with my own.

Brandon collapses over me, crushing me close. I've never felt anything as good as his heavy, muscular body squashing me deep into the air mattress. I sigh, and settle my face into the curve between his neck and shoulder. I stroke the supple, firm muscles of his back.

"We need a real bed next time," he says into my neck.

"Yeah. You moved this thing halfway across the room."

Brandon turns his head to see where we've fetched up. He grins as he lifts himself onto an elbow and strokes my face. "I wasn't too rough?"

"I loved every minute of it. Let's do it again."

He kisses me. "I love you." He looks down at me, the question plain in his honey-colored eyes.

"I love you, too." I reach up and pull Brandon's head down to mine, kissing him with all the passion that he alone ignites in me —and always will.

EPILOGUE

Jade

"Has it really been two years since we got married?" I ask Brandon as he pulls the Beemer up to the curb in front of a strip mall in Santa Monica. The sun is setting, and as we get out of the car, I feel a breeze, cool and kelpy with the unique smell of the California ocean, swirl my dress around my legs. "This seems like a goofy spot for our anniversary dinner."

Brandon grins. "I think you're going to like this." I laugh at the phrase we found a way to say a lot that first year we were together, and then the following year after we got married, and even more as time has gone on. He walks around the shiny silver car. "Do you trust me?"

"You know I do." I learned my lesson after that bumpy start— no one could love me more than he does.

"Good." He ties a kerchief over my eyes and takes my hand. "Right this way."

I cling to Brandon's arm as he leads me up the sidewalk to some sort of door. I hear him fumbling around with a key, a muttered curse—then he gets it open. "Wait here just a second."

I stand in the doorway, blindfolded, feeling vulnerable. I wrap my arms around myself as I feel another draft of air, this time from within—and it smells a little musty. Not like a restaurant. I hear some sounds from inside, a clunk. Crinkling.

We've been looking for a house to buy since we've been talking about starting a family now that I'm moving out of music videos into helping him with Forbes Talent. *Surely this isn't our house?* I didn't even see a scrap of yard anywhere nearby. My hands go damp. I wish I could wash them, and it makes me realize how much better I am. I hardly ever have that obsession any more.

"Okay." Brandon sweeps me up into his arms, making me gasp and giggle as he steps over the threshold. "You can take the blindfold off."

I lift the kerchief up off my eyes and look around from the haven of his arms. The lights are on in a carpeted waiting area, directly in front of the entrance we just came into. The waiting area is separated by a low seating ledge from a shining wooden floor that ends at a mirrored wall fronted with a barre.

Hanging from the barre is a long silver banner proclaiming, HAPPY ANNIVERSARY. A huge bouquet of peach-colored roses rests on the floor beneath the banner beside a bottle of champagne and two flutes.

"It's a dance studio," I say.

"Your dance studio," Brandon says. "Happy anniversary, honey."

I slide down out of his arms. "I can't believe this."

My lips feel numb. He's done some wonderful, amazing things in the time we've been together, but this... my own studio, to dance, to teach, to share with others.

"You like it?" Brandon's getting nervous at my lack of response.

I can't express my feelings in words. Instead, I take his hand

and lead him out onto the floor, placing his hand at my waist, mine on his shoulder. "I love you so much." We've been taking ballroom lessons together, and his waltz is already at least as good as mine. "Let's dance."

And as we move around the shining floor in perfect sync, I glance over at the vase of roses through a blur of tears. There will be thirteen of them.

I'm the lucky one, now.

Turn the page for a sneak peek of *Somewhere in Wine Country*, A Somewhere Series Secret Billionaire Romance Book 1

SNEAK PEEK

Meg

Gram had been gone a month now, and as much as I missed her, I was glad that she was in Heaven, and didn't have to sit with me on the back porch, look out across the dried-up grass to the vineyard, and watch the travesty of the foreclosure play out.

Tears prickled my eyes, and I smacked them away. "Stop it, Meg!"

Sir Henry Puddlejump, Grandpa's old Maine Coon, trotted up the back steps and yowled a greeting—just the distraction I needed. "Hey, handsome. Need something to eat?"

Sir Henry replied in the affirmative. An absolutely humongous cat, almost the size and fluffiness of a well-fed raccoon, Sir Henry didn't need to be fed twice a day, but I dared not resist his demands. He'd also earned his rewards—the cat had spent the last weeks of Grandpa's life on his bed with him and had fetched me when Gram had her heart attack and collapsed in the vineyard last month.

What a terrible month it had been. Yeah, I'd inherited Villier Vineyard, but I'd also been landed with the remains of Grandpa's cancer treatment medical bills, outstanding taxes, and a mortgage my grandparents had taken out to keep the vineyard going during the drought years in California. Operating a vineyard, even a small one that just grew grapes for other labels as ours did, wasn't a cheap operation.

Gram and I had got through Grandpa's illness, death and funeral leaning on each other. She hadn't said a word about how bad things were . . . and then *bam!* Heart attack. She was gone.

And I'd begun opening the bills.

I'd had no idea the vineyard had already been in foreclosure. I was reeling, with no time to do a thing about the upcoming auction at the Sonoma County Courthouse, already scheduled.

No wonder Gram had checked out for the afterlife.

I could sometimes feel her presence, a kind of sweet powdery rustle, as she watched me pack up the house, box her things to donate, and do what I could to get the fields and our generational family home ready for the gavel. "You know I tried, Gram," I said, petting Sir Henry as he rubbed his big furry body against my leg and purred like a chainsaw. "But I was too late to do anything."

I could almost hear her voice. "Don't blame yourself, Meg. Things were in motion long before you arrived."

But arrive I had, right after finishing a degree in teaching to prep for a career I wasn't sure was right for me. I'd been procrastinating on job hunting, hoping to reconnect with grandparents I remembered fondly from my childhood.

Gram, Grandpa and I fell in love on the steps of the big old farmhouse the day I arrived. There was no other word for the sense of homecoming and the rush of joy and endorphins I felt when they embraced me.

"You mean you fell in love," Gram had said. "I fell in love twenty-six years ago, when your mama brought you home from the hospital."

People said I looked like Gram, with my tall sturdy build,

wild reddish hair, freckly skin and hazel eyes. Certainly, I looked nothing like my pretty, petite, stylish mother. "Your mama took after Grandpa. He had many skills, for a skinny little Frenchman," Gram had said with a wink.

Great-Grandpa Villier had emigrated to California from France, with cuttings for our pinot noir grapes hidden inside a vest, along with enough money to buy the place during the wine desert years of Prohibition. Villier was a small operation at only eleven acres, but the vines, grafted onto acclimatized rootstock, were top quality.

Our farmhouse had been here much longer than the vineyard, and I loved every creaky board and sticky window jamb of its turn-of-the-century charm.

"No sense lollygagging," I told Sir Henry. "That won't hold off the inevitable. And I need every penny from the sale to get us out of debt."

I fed the old reprobate and left him muttering commentary into his Tender Vittles on the back stoop. I put on Gram's big straw hat, and headed out to mow the long, sloping lawn with its pools of shade cast by old-growth oak and walnut trees.

I was mowing the grass to make it pretty for the auction.

"Just push the damn mower, Meg." But every time I remembered what was happening tomorrow, I wanted to puke.

I couldn't do anything to change losing my family home. I could only mow the lawn and hope to have time to slap a coat of white paint on the porch before it got too dark.

Kane

I had a copy of the Santa Rosa Press Democrat open on my knees, an uncapped highlighter in my mouth, and the beginnings of a headache behind my eyes.

I hadn't planned to just plunge right into buying a vineyard. But I'd been driving around for days and applying for jobs all over Sonoma County, with no one even willing to give me a chance at pulling weeds in the fields, to start learning viniculture. "Harvard Business, huh? Don't need that here."

I was bummed. Seriously. Flea and I were sick of camping out of the back of the truck, pulling deep into the dirt roads of vineyards to crash at night.

The stupidity of my quest had begun to nag at me as I jotted notes in my logbook about the vineyards I'd approached: *La Crema. Hook and Ladder. Iron Horse.* Each time, nerving myself up, settling Flea in the truck with water, putting on my cleanest shirt.

Each time shot down.

But going home to Boston this soon, with my tail between my legs, wasn't going to happen.

The trouble with being the oldest son of billionaires was that you couldn't really talk about it to anyone. No one gave a shit about the perceived problems of someone who "had it all." My college buddy Dan had punched me when I'd tried to tell him about my existential angst. "STFO, bro. I'd say get a life, but you've already *got* the life."

As the oldest of the McCallum boys, I was supposed to set an example, which I'd done by anyone's measure. Mom and Dad had nothing to complain about: I'd been a star track athlete and class president at Andover, gone to my hometown Ivy League, and majored in business to take over McCallum Industries when Mom and Dad were ready to retire.

The issues had begun after graduation, when Dad gave me a small company to practice on: managing a strip mall just outside of Boston. *Ugh.* I hated it.

And then there was the breakup.

Hayley and I had met in college. She was smart, pretty and

sporty. Our parents knew each other from fancy fundraisers and whatnot. We dated, had mediocre sex, and I thought things would die a natural death—but near the end of senior year, Hayley told me it was time for an engagement announcement. "Everyone is hoping. They'll be so excited," she said. "Let's surprise our parents with a ring."

"Are you proposing to me?" My brows shot up. I liked Hayley, sure. But I wanted—something big. Something amazing. Something like the love my parents had—chemistry, passion, as well as teamwork.

I hated to say it about such a nice person, but Hayley bored me.

Hayley's cheeks got a little rosy. The girl never got flustered, though. "It would be a great partnership."

"Hayley, I think we've reached the end of the road. I'm not ready. Sorry if you thought that was where things were going."

I was wrong about her never getting flustered.

She turned bright red and balled her fists. "How dare you!" She spat. "You think you're the crown prince or something. Well, you're a lousy lay." She ripped off the silver bangle I'd given her for her birthday and threw it at my head. "You wasted my time."

She stomped off.

Lousy lay. Ouch. I could have sworn at least *she* had a good time—I believed in "ladies first."

I was done with women.

How could I trust that anyone wanted me, for myself, and not for the McCallum money?

And that had led me to the next big problem.

Our family were good people. We did good with our money. But the universe was skewed, and things weren't fair. I was the son of privilege, and I'd had every advantage available before I was even born. That said, it also felt like my future was already

241

mapped out, a dance with memorized steps, a part I'd been playing.

Looking down the line at what was ahead had made me claustrophobic to the point that I plotted my escape.

Dad was surprisingly cool about it when I nerved myself up to break the news that I was taking an extended road trip to figure out what was next for me. I'd already sold a bond and had seed money, my truck outfitted, and my camping gear. I was going all the way from Boston to California, and somewhere along the way, I'd find the perfect business to buy.

Dad's a big guy like me, six-three, with rough sailor's hands and the original dark blue eyes I inherited. "Pete, I get it. You know how I've always told the story about sailing around the world on the *Creamy Maid*, and meeting your mom on St. Thomas? Well, the part I never told you was that I left everything behind for three years while I was doing that. Your grandparents had just died, and I bailed on all the money and responsibilities of McCallum Industries. I sailed the world twice, and I lived on what I could earn with a skeleton crew to run the boat. I needed to know if I could even *make* it on my own. So, while I wish you didn't have to do this, I can't say I don't understand." Dad was the only one who called me Peter—I was named for both his and Mom's fathers, and even twenty-plus years after his parents' deaths in a plane accident, he seldom spoke their names.

"This won't work if it's not real." Mom's green eyes got a little watery as she put her hands on my shoulders. "I love you for being you, Kane. I'm just glad you finished college first. You may not want that MBA right now, but it's waiting for you anytime you might need it again."

My brother Colton told me I was nuts, and promptly took over managing the strip mall. Clearly someone had no problem with the family biz. David laughed his ass off and moved into my room because it had better light for his painting. Morgan just shook his head—our family inventor never talked much. Ben told his menagerie of strays and rescues what a nutjob I was. And Jesse? Jesse tried to stow away in my truck. He would have gotten away with it, too, if Flea hadn't sniffed him out.

I looked up as Flea woofed. We were camping in a grove of oaks at a county park, and he was wagging his tail in front of a gopher hole. "That rodent's not going to come out and play with you, buddy," I muttered.

I scanned the paper one last time. On the back page, I spotted an ad for a foreclosed vineyard up for auction at the Sonoma County Courthouse. The open house for the place was today. "Might as well check it out." I circled the address.

I whistled for Flea.

My boy was huge, and when he galloped at me, cheeks flapping, I could practically feel the earth shake. I named him Flea because (a) he's black, (b) he was the runt of a litter, and (c) he was supposed to be small. I'd adopted him as a rescue when he was a little fuzzy undernourished pup. They'd told me he was a terrier that wouldn't be more than fifteen pounds; a couple of years later, he was close to two hundred, and our best guess as to his breed was Great Pyrenees.

Flea hopped into the truck, I fired up the GPS on my phone, and we headed for Villier Vineyard.

Download and continue reading *Somewhere in Wine Country* now: tobyneal.net/WnCnwb

ACKNOWLEDGMENTS

Dear Readers,

I'm so happy you danced along with me for Jade's story! I danced in my younger years, and have been a huge fan of the *So You Think You Can Dance* reality show. Every interest I have eventually finds itself into my writing, so I enjoyed revisiting the intense drama of the best competitive dancing to hit TV, and inventing a show. By making this story a "retro" romance, I could include some of the artists and songs that defined the late 1980s and early 1990s, and to remember things like Walkmans and pagers and how easy it was for misunderstandings to happen in the age before cell phones.

The world has changed a lot since then, but finding love, in all its beautiful complexity, has not. As I was coming to the end of this book, I realized how much I care about these sisters and of the loving family they are building, and I wanted to write more—but *how*? I'd used up the family whose stories I wanted to tell!

Suddenly I realized that little Peter would be around twenty-eight in current times—and Pearl and Magnus's little one would be grown too! So we'll be fast-forwarding to the future, and you'll be meeting the next generation at a vineyard in a story called *Somewhere in Napa*. The Michaels family will go on! I hope you'll join me for their next adventure.

Much aloha from Maui,

Toby Jane

FREE BOOK

Read Rafe and Ruby's story FREE when you join my newsletter list and receive *Somewhere on St. Thomas,* Somewhere Series Book 1 as a welcome gift.

tobyneal.net/TNNews

TOBY'S BOOKSHELF

ROMANCES
Toby Jane

The Somewhere Series
Somewhere on St. Thomas
Somewhere in the City
Somewhere in California

The Somewhere Series
Secret Billionaire Romance
Somewhere in Wine Country
Somewhere in Montana
(*Date TBA*)
Somewhere in San Francisco
(*Date TBA*)

A Second Chance Hawaii Romance
Somewhere on Maui

Co-Authored Romance Thrillers
The Scorch Series
Scorch Road
Cinder Road
Smoke Road
Burnt Road
Flame Road
Smolder Road

PARADISE CRIME SERIES
Toby Neal

Paradise Crime Mysteries
Blood Orchids
Torch Ginger
Black Jasmine
Broken Ferns
Twisted Vine
Shattered Palms
Dark Lava
Fire Beach
Rip Tides
Bone Hook
Red Rain
Bitter Feast
Razor Rocks

Paradise Crime Mysteries Novella
Clipped Wings

Paradise Crime Mystery
Special Agent Marcella Scott

Stolen in Paradise

Paradies Crime Suspense Mysteries
Unsound

Paradise Crime Thrillers
Wired In
Wired Rogue
Wired Hard
Wired Dark
Wired Dawn
Wired Justice
Wired Secret
Wired Fear
Wired Courage
Wired Truth
Wired Ghost

YOUNG ADULT

Standalone
Island Fire

NONFICTION
TW Neal Pen Name

Memoir
Freckled

ABOUT THE AUTHOR

Toby Jane is the romance pen name for author Toby Neal, a mystery author who can't stop putting romance into all of her books! Toby Jane is the place where she gets to indulge her passion for happy endings, big families, and loving pets..

Toby also writes memoir/nonfiction under TW Neal.

Visit tobyjane.com for more ways to stay in touch!

or

Join my Facebook readers group, *Toby Jane's Romance Readers,* for special giveaways and perks.

Made in the USA
Columbia, SC
20 May 2021

38285531R00155